A Touch of Heat

Judy Mays

What the critics are saying...

ꟹ

Perfumed Heat

"PERFUMED HEAT is a short erotica, but nonetheless is packed with Ms. Mays' trademark "heat within a story" writing talent.... This reviewer loves the realistic characterizations Ms. Mays does with her werewolves, and the vivid erotic passions they feel.... Although a short story, this still leaves a reader feeling satisfied with the great ending, and then have one searching out more of Ms. Mays's books." ~ *Love Romances*

In the Heat of the Night

"Ms. Mays has done it again! … Kearnan is definitely the alpha male in this novel; his character is so complex he astonished me with his honor, morals, and courage. Serena is his equal…When Kearnan and Serena make love it is intense, passionate, and HOT! The heated love scenes were packed with surprises and depth that will captivate all of your senses and raise your room temperature. Judy Mays has created an erotic story that will titillate her readers with her explosive writing style. I for one will add this story to my home library and read it over and over again." ~ *Just Erotic Romance Reviews*

An Ellora's Cave Romantica Publication

www.ellorascave.com

A Touch of Heat

ISBN 1419950339, 9781419950339

Edited by Raelene Gorlinsky
Cover art by Syneca

This book printed in the U.S.A. by Jasmine-Jade Enterprises, LLC.

Trade paperback Publication January 2005

Content Advisory:

S - ENSUOUS
E - ROTIC
X - TREME

Ellora's Cave Publishing offers three levels of Romantica™ reading entertainment: S (S-ensuous), E (E-rotic), and X (X-treme).

The following material contains graphic sexual content meant for mature readers. This story has been rated E–rotic.

S-*ensuous* love scenes are explicit and leave nothing to the imagination.

E-*rotic* love scenes are explicit, leave nothing to the imagination, and are high in volume per the overall word count. E-rated titles might contain material that some readers find objectionable—in other words, almost anything goes, sexually. E-rated titles are the most graphic titles we carry in terms of both sexual language and descriptiveness in these works of literature.

X-*treme* titles differ from E-rated titles only in plot premise and storyline execution. Stories designated with the letter X tend to contain difficult or controversial subject matter not for the faint of heart.

Also by Judy Mays

ꟸ

Celestial Passions: Brianna
Celestial Passions: Sheala
Nibbles 'n' Bits (*Anthology*)
Heat: A Midsummer Night's Heat
Heat: Solstice Heat
Rednecks 'n' Rock Candy

About the Author

ꕥ

Living in a small town in Central Pennsylvania, Judy Mays spends the time she isn't teaching English to tenth graders as a wife and mother. Family is very important to Judy, and she spends a lot of time with her husband and children. Judy's pets are a very important part of her life, and she's had many over the years. Currently, Zoe the cat and Boomer the Lab mix help keep things hopping around the house.

Judy loves reading - especially romance, the "spicier" the better. After reading from more years than she cares to admit, Judy decided to try her hand at writing romantica is writing romance - and her wonderful husband of seventeen years provides plenty of motivation and ideas.

In the upcoming months, the tales by Judy Mays will contain werewolves, vampires, witches, and aliens from five planets on the other side of the galaxy. All of the heroes or heroines will fall madly in love and demonstrate their love in so very, very many ways.

Enjoy Judy's books, and after you've read one, she would love to hear what you think. Either stop by her website at www.judymays.com and sign her guest book or contact her directly at writermays@yahoo.com. She can't wait to hear from you.

Judy welcomes comments from readers. You can find her website and email address on her author bio page at www.ellorascave.com.

Tell Us What You Think

We appreciate hearing reader opinions about our books. You can email us at Comments@EllorasCave.com.

A TOUCH OF HEAT

By Judy Mays

PERFUMED HEAT

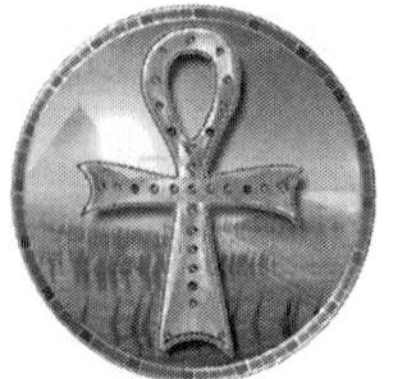

Chapter One

ꙮ

As they stepped into the crowded ballroom, Artemis groaned mentally and snagged his son's arm. Fool woman invited all of New York. "Is she here yet?"

Brendan scanned the crowded room. "You read the information in her dossier. I'd say she was probably the first one here. Sylvia James is not a woman to miss out being able to gloat over her good fortune."

Artemis snorted. Myriad scents, both intriguing and repulsive, swirled around the room, almost overpowering his senses. "Tell me again why we have to work with this particular woman."

Belle tucked her hand under his arm. "We've been through this, Father. It will be much easier to break into the women's fragrance market in partnership with an established company."

Artemis snorted again. "We managed fine with the men's cologne."

Before Belle could answer, Brendan said, "There she is with those other women by the buffet table."

Turning slightly, Artemis slowly perused the small group of women. "Which one?"

"The icy-looking blonde."

Artemis's gaze slipped past the tiny, dark-haired woman and the curvy redhead in gray to the blonde talking animatedly at an angry Amazon. Sylvia James looked every inch the successful businesswoman she was, from the top of her perfectly dyed platinum blond hair to the tips of her expensive Italian shoes. In her blue designer gown, she was the epitome of grace and elegance.

Artemis would sooner trust a weasel.

"Are you absolutely sure we can't find a better proposal from someone else?"

Brendan smiled and nodded at the city councilman who walked by. "Unfortunately, hers is the best proposal we've received. James Parfumes is a solidly established company with a firm percentage of the perfume market. We'd be fools not to accept."

"Watch yourself, Dad," Belle murmured into his ear. "She's seen us and is looking your way with a definite glint in her eye."

Raking the blonde with his gaze once again, Artemis remained unimpressed. "She doesn't interest me in the least, Belle. There's not a woman alive who can compare to your mother."

Belle laid her hand on his arm. "Dad, it's been…"

Artemis patted the hand Belle still had tucked under his arm. "More years than I want to remember, but then we've had this conversation before. Women simply don't interest me. Now, come along. Both you and Brendan say Sylvia James is the best choice to help set up our line of women's perfume. I may as well meet her and get it over with."

As her father pulled her forward, Belle glanced over her shoulder at her brother.

Brendan grinned and shrugged his shoulders. Belle could keep trying to fix their father up with all the different women she wanted, but it still wouldn't make any difference. There wasn't a woman on Earth to compare to the wolf their mother had been.

Still trying to escape the talkative grandmother, Moira watched as Belle and Brendan Gray escorted the man who had to be their father towards her boss. She'd conquered the urge to go right up to him and introduce herself. She had to be patient and wait for the opportunity to talk to him. Sylvia would certainly try to keep him at her side as long as possible now that she'd seen how good looking he was, even with his gray hair. When she'd first met Artemis's son Brendan in Sylvia's office, Moira had been initially surprised at his prematurely silver hair, but now that she saw his father, she decided it must be a family trait—for the men in the family, at least. Belle Gray had hair so black it had blue highlights, but Artemis Gray's hair was the same silver color as his son's.

Moira allowed her gaze to roam up and down his body. If she didn't know better, she'd think the Grays were brothers rather than father and son. Artemis was just over six feet tall, at least two inches taller than his son. His shoulders and chest, which tapered to a slim waist and hips, were broader than Brendan's too. His long legs ate up the distance as he led his son and daughter toward Sylvia.

When Artemis got closer, Moira was able to get a clearer look at his face. His long sliver hair was swept back off his high forehead and tucked behind his ears to fall softly to his collar. His face was strong with high cheekbones and firm chin. A bold nose over what looked like mobile lips dominated his face. Rather than simply walk across the room, he stalked with a loose, easy stride. And his stormy gray eyes moved constantly, sliding from one person to another, one face to another. He paused momentarily and said a few words to another of James Parfumes' competitors. After a quick nod, he moved forward again, his eyes now fixed on Sylvia.

A shiver danced up Moira's spine. Oh, to have eyes that intense fixated on her. Then she caught herself. Where did that thought come from? Artemis Gray was a means to an end, nothing more. It didn't matter to her how handsome or sexy he was.

Off to her left, Sylvia James hummed. "Oh my, my, my, my, my." Then she chuckled.

Moira frowned. She knew that laugh. Her boss had just decided who the next man in her bed would be.

Just as Moira was about to step to her boss's side, Artemis snapped his head up and inhaled. Both Belle and Brendan did the same. All three screwed up their faces as if they'd smelled something dead.

Nostrils flaring, Artemis stopped. Someone was wearing animal musk—too much of it—poorly mixed with the other ingredients of the perfume. Nor did it blend well with that person's personal scent.

Almost gagging, Belle coughed and stumbled.

Artemis tightened his hold on her arm until she caught her balance. Her nose had always been overly sensitive.

Sylvia James, a rapacious smile on her lips, stepped towards them. The tang of her perfume floated across the space between them and assaulted their senses, overpowering all other scents around them.

Eyes watering, Belle did gag.

Coughing, Brendan turned his head away.

Breathing through his mouth, Artemis held up his hand as Sylvia took another step. "No closer, Ms. James. Not only is the perfume you're wearing atrociously mixed, but it also contains animal musk. How many civets were killed for your company to make that perfume?"

Sylvia halted in midstride. However, the surprise on her face was quickly replaced by cunning as she lifted her hands and shrugged. "I don't know what you're talking about."

Artemis folded his arms across his chest and glared at her. "Liar. My nose is sensitive enough to tell you every ingredient in the perfume you're wearing. Civet musk is one of them. Our deal is off."

Anger rapidly replaced Sylvia's initial shock. Fists clenched, she dropped her arms to her sides and spat, "You wouldn't dare. I'll sue you for breach of contract."

Artemis shrugged. "Go ahead and try but first have your lawyers reread section five, clause three of the contract, the one about the agreement being null and void if we discover animal musk is used in the making of your perfumes." Spinning on his heel, he strode back across the room, ignoring the hushed whispers from the people who'd been standing close enough to hear their exchange.

Handkerchief held to her nose and mouth, Belle followed her father.

Hissing obscenities under her breath, Sylvia turned her attention to Brendan. "You don't know with whom you're fucking, you stupid fools," she threatened in a low voice.

Brendan bared his teeth in a toothy grin. His voice was just as low and much more menacing. "Fuck with us, Sylvia, and it will be the last fucking you ever do. And, according to your reputation, fucking is a major pastime. Cut your losses. We can and will ruin you."

After his warning, Brendan spun on his heel and followed his father and sister.

Moira reached her boss's side just as Brendan was leaving. "What happened, Ms. James?"

Hands shaking, Sylvia yanked a gold-plated cigarette case from her bag. After pulling out the first cigarette she touched and lighting it, she stabbed it into her mouth, inhaled deeply, then exhaled. She inhaled again and blew the smoke out. Eyes narrowed, she glared across the room at Artemis Gray and his children. "Fucking assholes thinks they can ruin me," she said in a low voice. "They have no idea with whom they're dealing. We'll see who ruins whom."

Moira waved away the cigarette smoke Sylvia blew in her face. "What happened? I thought everything was settled."

Sylvia took another drag from her cigarette. "Someone must have leaked the ingredients to this new perfume I'm wearing. Gray knew it contains civet musk. All of them looked down their noses at me as if I smelled like shit. "

Biting her tongue to keep from saying "I told you so" about the perfume Sylvia had personally developed, Moira glanced across the room. All three Grays were watching them. "Oh, the 'no animal' clause."

Mindful of the crowded room and the inquisitive glances, Sylvia kept her voice low. "You knew about that clause and didn't tell me! You stupid twit."

Clenching her teeth, Moira turned her head away—Sylvia's perfume really did stink—and bit back the reply her boss deserved. Instead, she controlled her temper and said, "I had all of the important clauses highlighted in the copy of the contract I gave you. And I did warn you that the Grays were opposed to using any ingredients that weren't derived from plants when you insisted on developing your new perfume."

Sylvia smiled at a state senator who ambled by. Her eyes scrutinized the crowd as she wondered who'd heard her exchange with the Grays, but her attention was focused on Moira. "Then why didn't you remind me? I would have worn one of our other perfumes tonight, and they never would have found out." She blew another mouthful of smoke into her assistant's face.

Coughing, Moira turned her face away. *Bitch. If Grandfather's medical bills weren't so expensive, I'd quit in a minute.*

Who's the woman Sylvia James is talking to?" Artemis asked.

Belle looked across the room. "The redhead? Her personal assistant Moira Archer."

"Poor kid's getting an earful from what I can see," Brendan interjected.

"She's hardly a kid, Brendan," Belle answered in a dry voice. "Don't worry about her. She's an adult and can take care of herself. Forget them. If we want to launch a line of women's cologne, we have to find a new partner; and we aren't going to get as good a deal from someone else."

Artemis listened with half an ear as his children discussed potential business partners or murmured greetings to various acquaintances. Artemis exchanged small talk when necessary, but most of his attention was focused on the woman Sylvia James was berating.

Dressed in a modest gray evening gown and with her auburn hair neatly coiffed in a French braid, she carried herself with a natural elegance Artemis had observed in very few women over the years. She stood with her back to him, so he let his gaze travel down her back. Slender waist, softly flared hips, trim ankles. Then she bent over slightly. The soft silk of her dress draped itself over a beautifully shaped behind.

When his cock stirred, Artemis started mentally. He hadn't had a physical reaction to any woman in more years than he cared to remember.

Sylvia lit her third cigarette. "I've heard enough of your excuses, Moira. It's your fault that the deal with Artemis Gray fell through. Just get out of my sight until I'm ready to leave before I fire you."

Temples pounding, Moira spun away from her boss and struck out blindly across the room skirting talkative groups, ignoring anyone who tried to engage her in conversation. *My fault! My fault the deal fell through! Bullshit. I'm sick and tired of taking the blame every time she screws up. I swear my resignation will be on her desk first thing in the morning. I have skills. I can get another good job. Grandfather and I will manage, somehow.*

Cocking his head to the side, Artemis watched as Moira Archer whirled and stomped away from her boss. She came closer, weaving her way through the crowd, obviously unmindful of her direction. Wisps of hair fluttered around her flushed cheeks, a flush that spread down her neck into the vee-shaped bodice of her dress.

She's very angry, Artemis thought to himself as he admired the way the soft silk of her dress draped over her breasts. *Sylvia probably blamed her for losing the deal with us.*

When Moira was close enough, Artemis stepped in front of her.

"Are you all right?"

She stumbled and stopped just short of plowing into his tuxedo-covered chest. Nostrils flaring, lips pinched together, she glared up at him.

Finally, Artemis got a good look at her face. She was not a classic beauty. Her nose had a bump in the middle. Her mouth was a tad too wide though her lips were probably full. It was hard to tell with them pressed into a thin angry line. Nor did her high cheekbones quite fit with her firm chin. But her eyes were what drew Artemis's attention. He had never seen such deep, emerald-green eyes.

As Artemis reached out to steady her, the delicate fragrance of lily of the valley embraced him. His senses tingled and he inhaled deeply. Then, along with the perfume, a far more subtle, enticing scent reached Artemis, a spicy, completely arousing scent. Moira was just entering the human version of heat.

The feral desire that had lain dormant in Artemis's soul for so many years roared to life, and the werewolf in him demanded sexual satisfaction.

Mine! Mate her! Now!

Like a fist in his abdomen, desire shot through Artemis. Blood rushed from his head to his cock, which immediately swelled and lengthened. His nostrils flared as he inhaled Moira's scent again. Why? Why this woman? A human woman's heat had never affected him before. He inhaled her scent again. Her rich, earthy aroma mixed with the perfume she wore enticed all his senses. *He had to have her*!

At Artemis's side, Brendan's head snapped up and his nostrils flared. Turning, he too stepped towards Moira.

Artemis's reaction was immediate. He clamped his hand down on his son's arm and hauled him back away from the young woman who stood before them.

Brendan tensed and shot a challenging glare at his father.

Artemis tightened his hand and snarled, "Mine."

Slowly, Brendan relaxed. Then he bowed his head to his father. "Yours."

Artemis released him, turned back to Moira, and looked deep into her eyes. He lifted his hand. "Come to me."

Chapter Two

ꟷ

Moira gawked at the hand only a few inches in front of her. Already angry from Sylvia's comments, her blood pressure rose even higher until her temples began to throb. *'Come to me'? Who the hell does he think he is? What am I, a dog?*

Ready to rip off a sharp retort, she jerked her gaze up to Artemis's face.

His head was bent towards her. Silvery-blond hair fell over his forehead and shadowed his eyes—smoky gray eyes that bore into hers, intense silver eyes that seemed to delve into her very soul.

Shivers danced up and down her spine. Her stomach somersaulted. The smooth satin of her bra began to irritate her nipples, and they hardened into tight nubs pushing against the silk of her dress.

Artemis's gaze dropped to her chest. Molten silver flashed in his eyes.

Desire shot into Moira's groin.

Artemis gaze returned to her face. The hand he held out to her didn't waver.

The sounds of conversation faded as Moira's breath caught in her throat. She licked her lips.

Golden sparks leaped in Artemis's eyes.

Moira finally breathed when her body demanded she do so. God, but the anticipation on his face was so intense, so dangerous, so—possessive. Nobody had ever looked at her like this before. Before she realized what she'd done, she stepped closer.

The spicy fragrance of Artemis's cologne wrapped itself around her and caressed her senses. Visions of his hands cupping and kneading her breasts, of her body naked and straining under his, her legs wrapped around his waist as he buried his rigid cock deep inside of her, appeared in her mind. Moisture seeped into her panties.

Moira inhaled. What was that scent he was wearing? His signature cologne, Artemis Gray? But there was something different about it, another ingredient. What was it? Why did she find it impossible to resist? She took another step.

The seductive spell Artemis was weaving around her was broken by Belle's voice.

Shivering, Moira wrenched her gaze from Artemis's. One glance at Brendan, and she jerked her attention away from him too. He looked just as intense, just as dangerous as his father.

Moira's gaze leaped to Belle. She only looked worried.

Belle touched Artemis's arm. "Father, are you all right?"

Artemis ignored her and kept all of his attention on Moira. His hand remained outstretched.

Moira glanced around the crowded room. People were beginning to stare. She saw Frank Gideon, the office gossipmonger, tap Sylvia on the shoulder and whisper something in her ear.

When her boss whirled around and motioned angrily towards her, Moira made up her mind. Choosing between Artemis Gray and Sylvia James was easy. Besides, she was in a crowded room. What could possibly happen?

Moira lifted her hand and placed it in Artemis Gray's.

Satisfaction leaped in Artemis soul as he closed his hand around Moira's. She had chosen him of her own free will. Now that he had her, he forced himself to relax, forced down the instinctive demands of his werewolf soul to pull Moira into his arms, to mount and mate her here before everyone. He forced down the urge to challenge every other male in the room, to demand that they acknowledge Moira was his. Artemis was an old and powerful werewolf. He'd learned to control his feral side a long time ago.

Lifting Moira's hand to his mouth, he brushed his lips across the back of her knuckles then tucked her hand under his arm. "Belle," he said, his gaze never leaving Moira's face, "introduce us."

Silence greeted his command.

Artemis glanced at his daughter.

Hands clenching and unclenching the strap of her evening bag, Belle was staring at him. A scent of confusion and surprise drifted to Artemis. He smiled. His daughter had nagged him for years to find another mate, but deep down, Artemis knew, she never expected him to. But then, neither had he.

Lifting his other hand, Artemis traced Belle's cheek then cupped her chin. "Don't worry, little wolf," he murmured. "Even though I never expected this, I must follow my instincts. You'll understand someday."

Artemis dropped his hand and turned to his son.

Tensed as if he were ready to run, Brendan was watching him warily. The slight scent of fear drifted around him. Artemis grinned. Seems like his cocky, self-confident son still recognized his father as Alpha.

Artemis reached out and squeezed Brendan's shoulder. "I'm sorry, but…"

The wariness fled and Brendan grinned, "You have to follow your instincts. Yeah, I know, I'll understand someday. And I'd never challenge you, Father."

Artemis chuckled. "At least not until I'm an old, old man, I hope."

Tucked against Artemis's side, Moira observed the byplay amongst Artemis and his children. Beneath her hand, his forearm relaxed then tensed then relaxed again. He seemed at ease, yet something about the way he had maneuvered her so that he stood between her and the entire room piqued Moira's curiosity. And what were he and his children talking about? Little wolf? What kind of pet name was that? Belle must have been a holy terror as a child. What kind of challenge was Brendan talking about? For a minute there, Moira thought Brendan and Artemis were going to fight.

Moira shifted and shivered. Standing this close to Artemis's big body was wreaking havoc with her senses. The spicy fragrance of his cologne seeped deeper into every pore with every breath she took. Every nerve she had felt overly sensitive. And it wasn't just his cologne. Somehow he *was* different. How? Deep down in her soul she knew he wasn't like any other man she'd ever met.

When Artemis looked down into her face again, her gaze went immediately to his mouth.

He lowered his head towards her. Beneath her hand, hard muscles of his forearm tensed again.

His scent teased her senses. She rose on tiptoe. One kiss. Just one kiss. She had to taste him.

"Moira, what do you think you're doing?" Sylvia James demanded in a strident voice behind her.

Moira felt as if a bucket of cold water had been dumped over her head. Shivering, she tried to step away from Artemis.

He placed his free hand over the one tucked under his arm and pulled her back against his side. Warmth spread up her arm. His hard thigh brushed hers.

Moira closed her eyes and snatched at her scattered wits. For the first time in six years, she was grateful for Sylvia's interference. Artemis was so appealing she'd been ready to make a fool of herself in front of a room full of people.

"As long as you're wearing that atrocious scent, Ms. James, don't come any closer," Artemis said before Moira could reply to her boss. "And, though it's certainly no business of yours, Moira has agreed to join us for dinner."

"She's my personal assistant. Of course it's my business," Sylvia spat from three feet away. "Moira, I forbid you to have dinner with them."

Moira's head snapped up as her anger surged. Her body, already on edge from Artemis's subtle sexual stimulation, had to release some pressure somehow. Sylvia James was the perfect catalyst. For the last seven years, Moira had put up with her boss's condescending comments and superior attitude. She was sick and tired of it, and she didn't care who heard her.

"You forbid me! You supercilious bitch. Last time I checked this was a free country. I can go where I want, eat dinner with whom I want, whenever I damn well please. I am not a slave. I am an employee, one who can quit whenever she wants to."

Conversations around them died.

A flash of fear appeared in Sylvia's eyes and her tone immediately became more cajoling. "Now, Moira, you're overwrought. Let's go somewhere and talk about that raise you wanted."

Another shiver of anger raced up Moira's spine. "A raise? You want to talk about a raise now?" She leaned forward.

Artemis squeezed her hand. His thumb slipped under her palm and began to trace delicate circles.

A different kind of shiver raced up Moira's spine.

Moira took a deep breath. Screaming at Sylvia James wasn't going to accomplish anything except entertain the avariciously nosy groups around them. There was only one thing left to say to her. Looking straight into her boss's face, she said, "I quit. My resignation will be on your desk in the morning." Moira looked up into Artemis's face. "I'm ready to leave any time you are."

With a nod, Artemis acquiesced. "Of course, my dear. Brendan, Belle."

"I'll fetch the car," Brendan said. He swept the room with a quick glance then walked away.

Sylvia's voice became desperate. "Moira, please…"

Moira opened her mouth, but Artemis squeezed her hand again. He directed his comments to her ex-boss. "Good night, Ms. James. The proper paperwork to dissolve any tentative partnership will be delivered to your offices tomorrow. Belle, Moira, shall we go?"

Moira smiled as Artemis led her away. She could hear her ex-boss sputtering something, but she ignored it. Finally, after seven years of Sylvia's snide comments, unreasonable expectations, and, at times, unqualified dishonesty, Moira had found the courage to quit her job. For one night at least, she was going to damn the consequences. Tomorrow she'd worry about how she'd support her grandfather.

Belle slowed until she was walking at Moira's side. "That was interesting. I didn't think Sylvia James would care so much about losing a secretary. What do you have that she wants so badly."

Moira knew her chuckle sounded spiteful, but she didn't care. "I have the formulas to all her best selling perfumes memorized."

Belle's eyebrows rose half way to her hairline. "Oh? Sylvia James didn't impress me as the type of boss who'd allow a secretary such vital information."

Moira's next chuckle was filled with malicious joy. "I developed them."

Moira didn't notice the sudden flare of satisfaction that gleamed in Belle's eyes.

Outside, Brendan was waiting next to a limousine.

Artemis helped Moira into the car then turned to his children. "You two don't mind taking a cab, do you?" He slid into the car without waiting for their answer and pulled the door closed behind him.

Chapter Three

ᘓ

Soft light illuminated the inside of the limousine as Moira settled back against the buttery-soft, leather cushions. The opaque window separating the driver from the passengers was closed.

Artemis slid into the limo, pulling the door shut behind him.

Brendan and Belle did not join them.

Moira's glance leaped from the closed door to Artemis. She was alone with him, and he was staring at her with that same intense expression that had been on his face earlier.

Trying not to seem too obvious, Moira inched across the seat away from him.

A predatory glint appeared in Artemis's hooded eyes.

Moira's breath caught in her throat. *Okay, what have I gotten myself into now*? "Where are Brendan and Belle?"

He leaned closer. "They're taking a cab."

Her back against the opposite side of the limo, Moira swallowed. "Oh. Ahhh, thank you for getting me away from Sylvia. You don't really have to take me to dinner."

Artemis stretched his arm out along the back of the seat behind her. "I know."

Lifting his other hand, Artemis rubbed his knuckles against her cheek. "Your skin is as soft as it looks." His fingers slipped behind her neck. Gentle pressure pulled her towards him. He bent closer. "You are a very lovely young woman." Then his mouth was on hers, his lips moving in a gentle, searching manner.

At first, Moira stiffened, but his kiss was so gentle and undemanding, she relaxed. Her lips softened and moved under his. Her hands drifted up to his shoulders. She sighed and inhaled his scent.

The fragrance of Artemis's cologne began to weave its spell again, enveloping Moira, seeping into her senses, tightening its hold on her psyche. How could cologne be so—seductive?

Pulling her lips from his, Moira asked, "What's the cologne you're wearing? It smells like Artemis Gray, yet it's different somehow. The bottle I bought doesn't have the same ingredients."

Artemis's hand remained on her neck. He slipped his fingers into the hair at the nape of her neck and began to trace delicate circles on her sensitive skin.

Her pulse beat erratically.

He caressed her cheek with his thumb. "It's a special blend for my personal use."

Breathless, Moira stared up into his eyes. Why was he so irresistible? "The audacity, to name a cologne after yourself."

"I'm an audacious man. I see what I want, and I take it."

Moira noticed flecks of gold in the irises of his gray eyes. Butterflies danced in her stomach. "What do you want?"

His stormy gaze was even more intense than it had been before. "You, Moira. I want you. Do you want me?"

Instead of answering, Moira inhaled. She'd been mixing scents since she was a girl but had never encountered anything like this blend of Artemis's cologne. Its uncanny fragrance was pure sexual stimulation, titillating and promising at the same time, an eclectic mixture of pine, sandalwood, cedar, and something else, something more subtle. Who would have ever thought those diverse scents could be melded into one compelling fragrance.

Opening her mouth, Moira inhaled and swallowed, using taste as well as smell to analyze the elusive ingredient in his cologne. Her eyes widened. "Aconite," she murmured. "Wolfsbane. That's your base. That's why I'm so attracted..."

As Artemis planted light kisses on Moira's neck and throat, her scent and taste settled around him like a warm blanket. The urge to mate grew stronger. "Why?" he murmured. "Why is aconite so appealing to you?"

Sighing, Moira closed her eyes and bent her head to the side, giving Artemis greater access. "Aconite is a base ingredient of the perfume I'm wearing now."

Artemis lifted his head from Moira's neck and stared down into her face. No wonder his reaction to her had been so strong. Aconite, wolfsbane, just a whiff of its pungent aroma had the werewolf in him howling for dominance. He should have known since he used it himself. Now he recognized the subtle scent enhancing the lily of the valley bouquet of her perfume, could isolate its sharp bite on his tongue from kissing her neck. The arid bite of the aconite-based perfume combined with the earthy smell of Moira's own sexual heat was an enticement impossible for Artemis resist. Lust surged through his blood. His balls contracted, and his cock expanded and stretched to its full size. His body demanded that he mate—*now*.

Sweat broke out on Artemis's forehead as he struggled to control the urge to tear Moira's clothing from her body, to pull her beneath him and plunge his cock in and out of her as hard and deeply as possible. He cupped Moira's face in both hands. "I want you, Moira," he repeated. "Do you want me?"

Moira opened her eyes and stared into his. Why fight fate? She'd wanted him since she first saw him stalking across the room. "Yes, Artemis, I want you." Lifting her head, she molded her lips to his.

Groaning, Artemis pulled Moira onto his lap, his left arm curled around her shoulders while he slid his right hand down her silk clad back and hip and thigh. He bunched her dress in his hand, pulling it up until he touched skin. When his hand slipped back up her thigh, her dress went with it. The combination of the cool skin whispering against her thigh followed by his warm, rough fingers had her shivering with anticipation. She wanted this man more than any she'd ever met.

Blood pounding in his ears, Artemis sucked Moira's tongue into his mouth. Still, he had his werewolf soul firmly under control. He wanted more than just a quick mating. He wanted to play first, to have Moira fall apart in his arms so he could watch her face as she came. Then he would take his pleasure—and bring her to climax again.

Repositioning Moira on his lap, he pushed her dress to the top of her thighs and slid his fingers between her legs. When his fingers reached her wispy silk panties, he tore them away.

Still in the first stages of her heat, she was only slightly swollen but wet, so very, very wet.

His cock strained against his trousers. He needed her to touch him.

Pulling his hand away from her thighs, Artemis jerked his pants open unmindful of the button that flew across the limo. He ripped his silk boxers and allowed his cock to spring free. Capturing one of Moira's hands in his, he guided it to his erection, shuddering when her fingers first teased its length—dancing and stroking down one side and up the other.

As her tongue mated with his, Moira gripped Artemis's cock and, slowly at first, then faster and faster, pumped it, her fingers squeezing, relaxing their grip, then squeezing harder again. Artemis groaned into her mouth when she palmed his first drops over the head over his cock. His balls tightened even more. The urge to explode built higher and higher.

"Easy, love. Not yet. You have to come for me first."

She didn't fight him when Artemis pulled her hand from his cock and slipped his hand between her thighs. He slid his fingers into her wet slit.

When Artemis slid his fingers between her legs, Moira moaned and spread her legs. Yes. This was what she wanted, what she needed. She stabbed her tongue into his mouth, mating it to his. When he slid first one finger then the second inside of her, she sobbed and thrust her hips against his hand.

"More, please, more."

Moira tilted her head back when Artemis's mouth left hers to trail kisses down her throat to her silk-covered breasts.

The sound of ripping cloth filled the limo as Artemis used his teeth to tear her dress and bra from her breasts. He sucked first one then the other nipple into his hot mouth, fingers sliding around and around her clit.

Moaning into his mouth, she thrust against his hand again.

He raised his head from her breast and stared into her face. "What do you want, Moira?"

Moira gripped his shoulders with both hands, straining against the fingers that swirled and dance between her thighs. "You," she sobbed. "Please, I need you inside of me."

Artemis's breathing grew harsher. "Like this?" He thrust two fingers into her.

A low keening moan escaped from Moira's throat as she arched into his fingers, her internal muscles clutching at the slippery digits as she ground her hips against his pumping fingers. The combined scents of Artemis's cologne, her own perfume, and the musty aroma of sex swirled and wafted around them, flooding Moira's senses. Her arousal spiraled.

Artemis sucked her nipple into his mouth and slid a third finger inside.

Her stomach muscles clenched, and her thighs shuddered. "Oh God, oh God, oh God."

Artemis lifted his head from her breasts and looked into her eyes. "Now, love, come for me now."

She shattered.

Before Moira stopped shuddering from her orgasm, Artemis sat up and settled back against the seat and pulled Moira onto his lap facing him. He had to be inside of her. Now! "Put your legs around my waist, love."

After she complied, he shoved her dress up around her waist, lifted her up, and dropped her onto his cock, thrusting into her deeply as he could.

"By all the gods, you're tight," he groaned. He buried his face in her neck, gripped her ass, and pulled her towards him as he began to pump.

Moira's hands slid down his shirt, bunching it in her fists. Buttons flew as she jerked it open and threaded her fingers through the hair on his chest. She pinched a nipple.

Artemis gritted his teeth as his balls burned. He didn't think his dick could get as hard and achy as it felt now. Still he fought against the pressure. His cock hadn't been inside of a woman for more years than he cared to remember so he was going to fight the urge to come and keep burying himself into Moira as long as he possibly could, allowing her slick muscles to grasp, clench, and squeeze him until she milked him of every drop of resistance. Only then would he allow himself his release.

Moaning, Moira arched her breasts towards Artemis's mouth as he impaled her on his cock. He was so very hot, so very, very hard. Her muscles stretched to accommodate his length then tightened to suck him further inside.

Sitting on Artemis's thighs with her legs around his waist, Moira shuddered as he stretched and filled her more than any other man ever had. She wiggled, and he slid deeper. She caught his rhythm, pulling him deeper and deeper with each thrust.

He lifted his face from her neck, lowered his head, suckled a nipple then nipped it.

A bolt of electricity seemed to jolt from her nipple to her groin. He suckled again and gyrated his hips, pushing his cock deeper.

Moira swiveled her hips and strained against him, sucking his cock even deeper into her body. She was hot, so hot. Pressure built. She threw back her head and screamed as another orgasm ripped through her.

This final tightening of her muscles was too much for Artemis. He slammed his cock into Moira as he felt his come erupt through his cock all the way from his balls.

Gasping for breath, tears rolling down her cheeks, Moira collapsed against Artemis's chest, inhaling the combination of cologne and male that comprised Artemis's unique scent. Never has she experienced such wild, uninhibited sex. At the moment, she didn't think she could even lift her head. Nuzzling his neck, she caught a bead of sweat on her tongue.

The warm rasp of Moira's tongue against his neck sent an electrical jolt into Artemis's still hard cock. He slid his hands around down over her ass and began to knead, lifting and separating each cheek then pushing them back together again.

Moira moaned and tightened her muscles around his cock.

Then Artemis realized the car had stopped moving.

Sighing, he slid his hands up to her waist, lifted her off of his cock, and set her on the seat next to him.

Sighing contentedly, Moira snuggled against him.

His still-erect cock jerked, and the werewolf inside of Artemis snarled with displeasure. He had yet to mount Moira and truly claim her as his; but, for the few minutes it would take to get into the house, he could wait.

Raking his fingers through his hair, Artemis grinned. Making love in the back of a limo—at his age. Once Brendan heard about this, he'd never hear the end of it.

Chapter Four

ꙮ

Lifting his hips, Artemis slid his cock back into his trousers, tucked the ripped edges of his boxers inside, and pulled up the zipper. He pulled his shirt together as best he could and tucked the tails into his pants.

Moira's bare breast brushed against his arm, and the werewolf in his soul leaped for control.

Artemis stifled its rebellion with a surge of will.

Moira was stretched out on the seat next to him, her eyes closed, a slight smile on her face. Wisps of auburn hair curled against her cheek and neck. Her dress was still around her waist. Her nipples were hard buds, and the ruddy curls at the juncture of her thighs seemed to glow with a fiery light all their own.

Artemis shifted to accommodate his erection. If they didn't get out of the car now, he'd have her all over again.

"Moira, we're home."

She opened her eyes and smiled.

A fierce jolt of possessiveness surged through Artemis as he stared into her eyes. Home. She was his! No other man would ever have her again.

As Moira stared into Artemis's face, the fog from her multiple orgasms vanished from her mind. *Home? Whose home? I thought we were going out for dinner.*

She pushed herself up, and her naked butt sank into the soft leather cushions. Two scraps of scarlet silk lay next to her on the seat. Artemis had ripped her panties in two.

He'd ripped the top of her dress and bra, too. *No man has ever been so excited about making love to me.*

Moira glanced down and warmth rushed into her cheeks. Her breasts were fully exposed. What's more, her dress was around her waist. She pulled it down and covered her breasts with her hands.

Artemis chuckled. "I've already seen your breasts, love, and kissed and sucked them.

Moira flushed even more. "Maybe you have, but I don't intend to get out of the car half naked so every other Tom, Dick, and Harry can get an eyeful."

Grinning, Artemis shrugged out of his coat. "Put this on."

Rose-colored nipples peaked in the cool air as Moira slipped her arms into the coat and pulled it tight around her body.

Once Moira had wrapped his jacket around her torso, Artemis opened the door and stepped out. Motioning the driver away, he held out his hand.

As Artemis helped her out of the car, she looked around. Warmth spread from her chest to her face when she saw the driver staring at her, an amazed look on his face.

God, I can't look that bad, can I?

His hand in the small of her back, Artemis guided her into the modest brownstone before them.

Once inside, an elderly man met them.

"May I take, ah... your coat, Miss?" he asked in a dumbfounded voice.

Moira flushed again. *Damn, I haven't blushed this much since my first gynecological visit.* "Ah, no thank you. I'm a little chilly. I'll keep it."

Behind her, Artemis chuckled. "That's all, Paul. Go to bed. It's late."

"But Mr. Brendan and Miss Belle..."

"Can take care of themselves. You're tired. Go to bed."

Paul's shoulders sagged a little and he nodded. "Very well, Mr. Artemis. Breakfast at the usual time?" he asked as he walked away.

"I'll let you know."

Momentarily, Paul stopped, half turned, then reconsidered. He disappeared down a dark hallway.

Moira glanced at Artemis. "Why is everybody staring at me like I have two heads?"

"Because I've never brought a woman home with me before this."

Her mind cleared more. "That's right. You're a widower." Then the full meaning of his words struck. "You haven't ever brought a woman home before?"

Artemis stepped closer. "I haven't made love to a woman since before Myste died."

Moira felt her mouth drop open. She snapped it closed. "You haven't had sex since your wife died? My God."

Artemis smiled a toothy grin. "The gods had nothing to do with it. I've never met a woman who appealed to me more than Myste."

Moira stepped back away from the intensity in his eyes and swallowed. "She had a beautiful name."

He nodded. "She was beautiful, far more beautiful than any woman—until now."

"Now?"

Artemis grinned. "I finally found a woman to take Myste's place." Scooping Moira into his arms, he strode into the dark hallway.

"Hey!" Moira yelped as she wrapped her arms around his neck. "Where are you taking me?"

"To bed."

"But I'm hungry."

"We can eat later."

Artemis's mouth descended on hers. His lips, mouth, and tongue cajoled, tempted, and teased her into silence.

Lost in the intensity of his kiss, Moira stopped thinking and simply enjoyed the physical sensations racing through her body.

His tongue dancing and swirling with Moira's, Artemis easily negotiated the dimly lit hallway until he got to his door, which he kicked open then shoved closed with his hip. At last, Moira was here in his rooms, his den.

The jacket she wore had fallen open, and her hard nipples stabbed his chest. Her short gasps and moans fired his passions higher.

Artemis inhaled, and the combined scent of her heat and the aconite base of her perfume swamped his senses. Fire exploded in his soul, and the werewolf in him asserted its power. The woman in his arms was in heat, and instinct told him to claim her, mate her before another male could do so.

Artemis slid his arm out from beneath Moira's legs, cupped her behind, and pulled her hard against his erection. His tongue circled her mouth as his kisses became more demanding, more dominating. He slid his hands up her back, bunched the suit jacket Moira was wearing, and tore it in two. Yanking the ripped halves from her shoulders, he dropped them to the floor. Artemis jerked what was left of her dress up and grabbed her ass cheeks, gripping each cheek as he lifted and rolled them. He thrust his thigh between her legs.

Lifting his head, Artemis stared down into Moira's flushed face. Her lips were swollen from his kisses; her eyes were unfocused. Both hands clasped tightly around the edges of his shirt so that her fingers brushed against the hot skin of his chest. He shuddered with the urgency to mate.

"Mine," he growled into her ear. "You're mine." Burying his face in her neck, he nipped her.

The sharp nip on her neck jolted Moira out of her sensual haze. The second, sharper nip goaded her into action. She jerked out of his arms and rubbed her neck. "Hey, that hurt."

Artemis reached for her and growled. "Come back to me."

"Not if you're going to bite me again, I won't."

Artemis's eyes were a dark, steel gray as he took a step towards her. "Moira, submit."

"Submit? Submit!" Moira fisted her hands on her hips. "What kind of masochistic bullshit is that? Listen, Artemis, this is the twenty-first century. Women do not submit to men."

"Mine does."

"Yours! I'm not your woman. We had some great sex, but that doesn't mean I belong to you. I don't belong to any man, and I never will."

Golden sparks jumped in Artemis's stormy eyes. "You belonged to me the first minute I smelled you."

"Smelled me? What kind of crazy comment is that? I don't smell. What is it with you?"

Artemis's nostrils flared. "Your scent is unique. You don't smell like other women, even under your aconite-based perfume."

Moira snorted. "More than human. Now I know you're nuts. I'm outta here." She shifted on her feet, ready to walk past him.

Artemis crossed his arms over his chest and smiled condescendingly. "Naked?"

Yanking the edges of her bodice together, Moira stamped her foot. Damn him. She couldn't leave like this. If she didn't get arrested for indecent exposure, some nutcase would rape her.

"Give me one of your shirts to wear, and I'll be fine."

"No."

Moira gritted her teeth. "No? You're the one who ruined my dress. You owe me."

Artemis's white teeth flashed. "You weren't exactly complaining."

Moira stomped her foot again. The heel broke on her shoe, and she staggered forward.

Artemis caught her before she fell.

"Let me go," she snarled.

Conquering the urge to simply throw her onto the bed and mount her, Artemis dropped his hands. Moira's denial of his advances had struck a nerve. He just couldn't overpower her and force himself on her. Werewolves didn't rape their mates. Moira was feisty, an alpha female in her own right. She'd be the perfect mate, but she had to accept and submit to him freely.

Moira staggered again and fisted her hands in his shirt to regain her balance.

Her dress gaped open, giving him a nice view of her breasts.

He grinned down at her. "Need any help?"

"No, damn it. Just get me some clothes and call me a cab."

Shaking his head, Artemis continued to grin and stared down at her. She was barely half a foot away. Her scent enveloped him.

She stomped the foot with the broken heeled shoe. "Don't just stand there, moron."

Artemis locked gazes with her. "Marry me, Moira."

Chapter Five

ஐ

There was an audible click when Moira snapped her jaws shut. "What!"

Artemis's expression became more intense. "Marry me."

Moira blinked. *He's crazy.* "Why?"

"Because I want you to."

"We only met a few hours ago. We don't even know each other."

"I know enough."

She shook her head. "No. That's impossible. You don't know anything about me except that I'm a good fuck."

Snarling, Artemis grabbed Moira's arms and shook her gently. "You will not degrade yourself like that."

Moira wrenched free. "You will not tell me what to do, and I wouldn't marry you if you were the last man on Earth."

Artemis chuckled. "But I'm not a man, love."

Moira snapped her mouth shut on the retort she was about to deliver. *Yep, certifiably nuts.* "Not a man? Then what the hell do you think you are," she asked in a derisive tone, "a vampire? That's why you bit my neck isn't it. Well, I have news for you buster. Vampires don't exist outside of sensationalist Hollywood movies and TV shows or trashy romance novels."

Artemis threw back his head and roared with laughter.

Her anger finally getting the better of her, Moira slammed her fist into Artemis's stomach.

He didn't flinch.

Pain exploded in Moira's fist and ran up her arm. Tears flooded her eyes as she shook her hand. Shit, but Artemis's abdomen was harder than some doors she'd run into. She glanced up.

He was grinning at her again. "Did you hurt yourself?"

"Yes, I hurt myself, moron," Moira snapped between blinks to clear her eyes, "but you need a doctor more than I do if you keep thinking you're a vampire."

"I'm not a vampire, love, but I'll be happy to introduce you to one if you'd like. There are a few I trust."

Moira's gaze darted around the room. Artemis didn't seem violent, but he was obviously not completely right in the head. Ah, a chest of drawers. There'd be something in there she could wear so she could leave.

"Yeah, well, another time, maybe." She turned away from him.

Artemis grasped her arm, gently. "I'm not a vampire, Moira, but I'm not completely human either."

She looked back over her shoulder. His eyes were now the color of morning mist. What are those golden sparks that keep appearing and disappearing in his eyes? "Are you trying to tell me you're an alien? Why would an alien from another planet come to Earth just to sell men's cologne."

Artemis's nostrils flared, and his eyes darkened. He was beginning to get angry again.

Moira bit her bottom lip. *Shit, girl. Can't you just shut up while you're ahead? He's bigger and stronger than you are.*

"Maybe it's better if I just showed you." Artemis let go of her arm and stepped back a few paces.

Moira blinked.

Artemis's figure was blurring.

She blinked again.

A swirling gray mist had surrounded him. The trousers and ripped boxers Artemis had been wearing dropped out of the mist to the floor. Then, the mist was gone and a silvery gray wolf sat before her.

Moira swallowed and closed her eyes. When she opened them, the wolf was still there. She closed her eyes again and kept them closed. "Damn it Artemis, what kind of tricks are you playing now?"

No tricks, Moira. Open your eyes. I'm sitting right in front of you. I'm a werewolf.

Moira opened her eyes.

The wolf stood, stretched, and paced towards her.

She tried to run, but her feet refused to obey her.

When the wolf reached her, it pushed its head, which just happened to be chest high on her, under her hand.

I'm not a figment of your imagination, Moira. I'm real. You can touch me.

Involuntarily, Moira's fingers curled into the silvery white fur on the wolf's head, fur far softer and silkier than any she'd ever felt on a dog. She swallowed. Her knees began to tremble, and she found herself sitting on the floor looking up into the wolf's face.

It swiped her cheek with its tongue.

Moira blinked and began to tremble, slowly at first, then more violently. She closed her eyes and cupped her head in her hands. "This isn't real. This can't be real. I was in a car accident. That's it. I'm lying in a hospital bed in a coma dreaming all this. That's it. I'm in the middle of a nightmare."

Silvery mist swirled again, and Artemis knelt before her. "You aren't dreaming, Moira. I am a werewolf, and I want you to be my mate."

The sound of a clock ticking reached Moira's ears. Tick tock, tick tock. Slowly, the sounds of the clock faded away. The room became blurry, then completely black. With a sigh, Moira sank slowly to the floor.

Cursing silently, Artemis caught Moira before her head hit the floor. Who'd have thought that someone this feisty was a fainter.

Rising, he laid her on the bed then leaped to the door and yanked it open. "Belle, get up here and bring an ammonia stick. Moira fainted."

Leaving the door open, Artemis returned to the bed.

"What did you do to her?" Belle demanded as she bustled into the room followed by Brendan.

"Told her I was a werewolf," Artemis answered indignantly. "I didn't think she'd faint."

Belle huffed. "What did you do? Say 'Oh, by the way, I'm a werewolf' and just *change*?"

Artemis bared his teeth and growled.

Totally unintimidated, Belle shoved Artemis out of the way. He was her father. He'd sooner chew off his own paw than hurt her.

As the odor of the ammonia permeated her senses, Moira was forced to leave the safety of oblivion and open her tearing eyes. Coughing, she pushed Belle's hand away. Blinking to clear her vision, she focused on the people around.

The obvious admiration and simmering lust in Brendan's eyes had her pulling the pillow from beneath her head and covering her body.

Snarling, Artemis leaped across the bed and grabbed his son's shirt. "She's mine!"

Brendan immediately hunched his shoulders and bowed his head. "Sorry, Father, but she's so—naked."

"Get her some clothes, Belle," Artemis snapped. "You—out," he added for Brendan's benefit.

Artemis's handsome son tossed a quick grin to Moira and said, "Welcome to the family." Spinning around, he hurried from the room.

Laughing, Belle followed him.

Brendan's comment had Moira gathering her scattered wits. *Welcome to the family. No way. No way in hell. I am not marrying a werewolf.*

Settling himself on the bed next to her, Artemis smiled. "Yes you will. I've chosen you for my mate. You'll agree."

Shit, can't I even keep my thoughts secret?

I'll teach you how if you want me to.

"Get out of my head, damn it!" Edging towards the other side of the bed, Moira shook her head. "Look, I'm honored and all that, but I really don't think it would work. I'm human. You're a werewolf. Two different species."

"When you have my blood, you won't be completely human any longer either."

A lead weight settled in Moira's stomach. Her voice squeaked. "Blood?"

Artemis chuckled. Moira was white as a sheet. "You aren't going to faint again are you?"

Her voice was stronger. "I have never fainted in my life. And drinking your blood is not an option because I'm not going to marry you."

Grinning, Artemis shook his head. "You don't drink my blood. You'll have a transfusion. A pint of my blood won't turn you into a werewolf, but it will—enhance—your current DNA. Your senses will be sharper, you'll be faster, stronger, and you won't have to worry about catching most of the diseases known to man. About the only thing you won't be able to do is change into a wolf."

Moira began to tremble. He was not taking no for an answer. "Why me?"

Artemis reached out and smoothed an auburn curl behind her ear. "I told you. You're the first woman I've met who erases Myste from my mind."

Moira twisted the edge of the pillow case in her hands. "But wouldn't you rather marry another werewolf like Myste?"

"Myste wasn't a werewolf. She was a wolf."

Moira remembered to breathe a minute later. "A wolf. You were married to a wolf?"

Artemis stretched out on his side. "Not married to, actually. Mated to. I was uncomfortable, restless with my human life. Life as a wolf is so much simpler. Hunt, eat, sleep. Then I met Myste and understood where I belonged. She accepted me as her mate. Life was bliss."

Artemis rolled onto his back, laced his fingers behind his head, and closed his eyes.

Moira was ready to slip off the bed. She glanced towards Artemis and stopped.

His entire body was tensed, and his forehead was wrinkled. But it was the expression of complete misery on his face that stopped her from leaving.

"What," she swallowed, "what happened?"

"When our cubs turned five months old, Myste was shot by a poacher."

Sympathy washed the fear from Moira. "Oh, Artemis, I'm so sorry."

When he opened his eyes, a single tear rolled down his cheek. "If it hadn't been for the cubs, I'd have died too."

"Belle and Brendan?"

He nodded. "And Melody, Garth, and Kearnan."

Moira couldn't keep the surprise from her voice. "There are more than Belle and Brendan."

"There were five in the litter all together. Myste was such a good mother, all of the cubs survived."

"Belle and Brendan's mother was a wolf? But why do they look human?"

"They got human DNA from me. Most wolves consider themselves superior to humans, and even those with werewolf blood rarely ever consider learning how to harness their power and change into humans. However, my cubs decided they had to learn to keep me alive."

"Were they right?"

A sad smile appeared on Artemis's face. "Yes. Without Myste, I didn't want to live."

Moira leaned closer and punched him in the shoulder. "Why you selfish bastard! Your babies were five months old when their mother died, and all you could think of was yourself? How could you do that when they needed you more than they ever had. And you want me to marry you? I'd sooner marry a vampire."

Turning away from Artemis, Moira rolled off the bed and strode to the open door where she grabbed the clothes Belle was carrying.

"Your father needs a good kick in the ass," she snapped. "If I were you, I'd use spiked heels."

After shimmying out of what was left of her dress, Moira tugged on the jogging suit Belle had brought and slid her feet into the sneakers. "Where's a phone? I want to call a cab."

"There's one on the way for you now."

Moira paused as she stepped through the doorway. "Thank you. It was—interesting meeting you, Belle. I hope you don't take it the wrong way when I say I hope I never see any of you again."

Belle simply grinned. "By the time you get downstairs, the cab will be there. I'm glad I met you, Moira. I'm looking forward to seeing you again."

"Don't hold your breath," floated back through the hallway.

"Why did you call her a cab?"

Belle turned back to her father. "She has a lot to think about, Father. And she couldn't do that with you breathing down her neck."

Mist formed on the bed then drifted across the room to where Artemis's trousers were heaped on the floor. The mist settled over them. It dissipated, and Artemis reappeared wearing his pants.

"Showoff," Belle said.

Chapter Six

ꟸ

Moira dropped the spare key usually hidden in the false rock next to the front porch on the hall table. She'd been in such a hurry to get out of Artemis's house, she hadn't even grabbed her purse. Well, he could keep it. No way was she going back there to get it. Staring at the key, she stuck her hand into the pocket of the sweat pants Belle had given her to wear and pulled out the business card she'd found there. Midnight black with one line of silver printing next to a wolf's head. Artemis Gray's private phone number.

"Is that you, Moira?"

"It's me, Granddad. Why aren't you in bed?"

Sighing, she headed for the living room. Maybe it was good he wasn't in bed. If anyone could make some sense out of the outlandish story she had to tell, it would be her grandfather.

When she stepped through the door, her eyes automatically zeroed in on the wheelchair sitting next to the fireplace. It was empty.

"I'm over here on the sofa, lass. Got tired of sitting upright waiting for you, and fell asleep on the sofa. It's not midnight yet. Either you're coming home too early or too late."

Flopping down onto the sofa, Moira raked her fingers through her tangled hair, grimacing when they caught in a snarl. "Too late by far, Granddad."

"Do you want to be talking about it then?"

Moira glanced over at her grandfather. His body may have withered over the years, but his mind was still sharp behind his piercing blue eyes. No matter how busy he'd been, he'd always taken the time to listen to her problems and offer advice. Moira felt her lips twitch. Some advice. It had almost always entailed her having to figure things out for herself. Ah well, may as well grab the bull by the horns. Granddad's reaction would be interesting.

"I met a werewolf tonight."

A smile curved his lips. "Did you now? And did he have big teeth?"

Moira relaxed more. "Very big teeth."

"And did he try to bite you then?"

Moira rubbed her neck. "He didn't *try* to bite me. He did bite me."

Her grandfather's smile became a frown. "Nibbles or real bites?"

Moira shivered as the memory of Artemis's nibbling kisses changed to sharper nips. "Well, he didn't really bite me. I mean he didn't break the skin. More like nips. Yeah, sharp nips."

He lowered his head and stared at her over his glasses. "And were you having sex with him when he nipped you?"

Heat erupted into Moira's face. "Grandfather!"

"I'm not blind, lass. Those weren't the clothes you were wearing when you left earlier. Now how is it he let you leave?"

"Let me leave?" Moira gawked at her grandfather. "You mean you believe me?"

"Of course, I do. You haven't married yourself off to a human, so it was only a matter of time until you found one of the Others, or one of them found you. I always thought it would be one of the Fae, though, since you've more of their blood. But then, you've been wearing that aconite-based perfume for the last few months. It was only a matter of time until one of them found you."

"Found—me?" she sputtered.

"Aye, your grandmother was half Fae, you know. I've only a bit of werewolf blood from my grandfather's grandfather. It had to be the wolfsbane."

Her heart was thumping in her ears. "Your grandfather's grandfather?"

"Aye. He was from northern Wales. There was a village there where humans and werefolk mostly got along. Might be gone by now."

It was heard to breathe. "Mostly—got along?"

Her grandfather nodded and continued to smile at her.

Speechless, Moira stared at the old man who had raised her since she was eight. Fae blood, werewolf blood? What was he talking about?

A log snapped and sparks shot up the chimney.

Moira leaped to her feet and planted herself in front of her grandfather. "Seamus Patrick O'Brien, are you crazy? Did you fall and hit your head today?"

Seamus cocked his head and smiled a gentle smile. "No, Moira, I'm not crazy, and I didn't fall and hit my head. Everything I'm telling you is the truth. Fae, werewolves, elves, and many more do exist though they do their best to blend in with normal humans."

"Why didn't you tell me this before?"

"Would you have believed me?"

Moira wilted onto the footrest before the sofa. "No. Who would?"

"Exactly. Now, what was his name, your werewolf?"

Moira snorted. "He's not my werewolf."

Seamus leaned forward and patted her knee. "I'm afraid he is yours, lass, and you're his."

Artemis's *'Mine'* echoed in her mind.

"What do you mean?"

Seamus sighed and leaned back. "Werewolves are like wolves. They mate for life unless their mates die young."

Moira swallowed. "His did."

Seamus nodded. "An older male, one who's been mated before. He'll have no doubts about you then."

"What do you mean, no doubts."

"Until you came along, he probably didn't notice other women—human or werewolf. He'd been mated once, for what he thought was life. She meant everything to him. That's how werewolves are, completely faithful to their mates often even after a mate dies. I have enough of their blood to know I'd never want another woman after your grandmother died. You were probably as much of a surprise to him as he was to you."

Stormy gray eyes appeared in her mind. *I haven't made love to a woman since before Myste died.*

"Moira. Moira?"

Her grandfather's voice penetrated.

"What?"

His voice was very gentle. "What about you?"

"What do you mean?"

"How do you feel about him?"

Moira shoved herself up and began to pace. "How do I feel about him? I didn't even know him twenty-four hours ago. How can I possibly feel anything for him?"

"You felt enough to make love with him."

"So?"

"Moira, I've never pried into your private affairs, but gentlemen callers have been few and far between around here. And those few you did introduce to me didn't have you falling into their beds the same night. I know you better than that. This werewolf is different, and you know it. Best if you admit it to yourself and not fight your own nature."

"What would you know about it?"

Seamus laughed. "My Da didn't tell me about our werewolf blood until a certain half Fae came floating about the house. Seems the Fae and werefolk didn't see eye to eye. He didn't want me seeing her anymore."

She sank onto the sofa next to him. "But you married Gram."

"Aye, I did, after almost a year of pure misery. My soul knew she was right for me, and I suffered every day I stayed away from her. I don't want you to make the same mistake."

"But Granddad. I don't even know Artemis."

"Artemis? Artemis Gray of the new men's cologne?"

Moira nodded.

"Well, now. Who would have thought *he* was a werewolf." He patted her knee. "Don't fight your instincts, Moira. They'll not lie to you. If he's your one true mate, your heart will know."

Moira dipped her head and sighed. She had been drawn to Artemis as soon as she'd first smelled the cologne he concocted. When she'd first seen him, the urge to meet him had gotten stronger. And when he touched her, she didn't want him to let her go.

Seamus patted her knee again.

She looked up.

The twinkle in his eye was impossible to ignore.

"What?"

"No matter how often your grandmother submitted to me, she still led me about like a bull with a ring in his nose. To a female werewolf, submission is the acceptance of a mate, nothing more. You need a strong mate, Moira, someone whose spirit is as strong as yours whether he be human or werewolf. You're a strong-willed woman, an alpha. If he weren't strong enough to hold you, you'd not think twice about him."

Moira rose. "I—I need to think, Grandfather. This is all so—strange."

"Go to bed and sleep on it. You'll feel better in the morning."

"Do you need anything?"

Seamus waved her away. "Be off with you, lass. I can manage to get myself to bed."

The adrenaline fueling the righteous indignation that had carried Moira home was gone. Her brain was spinning with everything her grandfather had told her, and she was exhausted.

Great sex will do that to you, an insidious voice in her head whispered.

Moira bent over and kissed her grandfather's head. She really did need to get some sleep. She'd worry about all of this in the morning.

* * * * *

"I don't care what you have to do but I want her at this address tomorrow, understand?"

The bald man looked at his companion and nodded.

"Here's her address. Her grandfather lives with her. He's confined to a wheelchair. Make sure she hears you threaten him, but don't hurt him—or her, or she won't cooperate."

Another nod.

"Well, don't just stand there. I'm paying you good money. Go get her."

Both men turned away and slipped silently through the door.

Sylvia James patted her perfectly coiffed hair and smiled. Moira Archer would remain in the employ of James Parfumes one way or another, whether she liked it or not. She was a genius with perfume formulas, more so than any of the so-called chemists employed by the company, and Sylvia wasn't going to lose her to a competitor. Once Moira understood just how—perilous—her grandfather's condition was, she'd cooperate.

Chapter Seven

ꟃ

Yawning, Moira pulled the belt tighter around her silk robe and stumbled into the kitchen, following the aroma of freshly brewed coffee. Thank goodness Granddad had set the automatic timer because she really needed caffeine. Grabbing a mug from the cupboard, she set it down and filled it to the brim. No cream today. She needed it black.

Mug cradled the mug between her palms as she sank into a chair by the table. Sipping the hot coffee she grimaced. It was stronger than usual, but the bitter taste did wake her up. Soon the caffeine would give her the energy she needed to get through the morning. Goodness knows, she didn't get any sleep last night. All she did was toss and turn and think about Artemis.

Damn it, what was she supposed to do? Him being a werewolf aside, she'd just met him. How could she agree to marry a man she barely even knew?

Outside the open kitchen window, a bird began to sing.

"Oh shut up. What the hell do you have to sing about anyway?"

"Ouch, lass, but is that any way to be talking on such a fine May morning?" Seamus asked as he slid shut the glass door that opened onto the patio behind their house. "The sun is shining, the flowers are blooming, and love is in the air."

Moira scowled at her grandfather. "If I want your opinion, I'll ask for it."

He grinned. "You already asked last night. I'll not be butting into what isn't my business now then, will I?"

Smiling in spite of herself, Moira shook her head. Granddad always knew what to say to make her smile.

She pushed herself up out of her chair and turned towards the coffee pot. "Do you want some coffee?"

The sound of shattering glass answered her.

Moira spun around to find broken glass from the door sparkling on the floor, and a huge linebacker of a man wearing a black ski mask holding a gun to her grandfather's head. Another even larger man in a blue ski mask stood just behind him, his attention divided between her and their backyard.

"What do you want? Please don't hurt him. I'll give you all the money we have in the house."

The man with the gun shook his head. "We don't want any money, lady. We're here for you." He motioned with his gun. "Let's go."

Moira stiffened her spine and drew herself up to her full five foot three inch height. "I'm not going anywhere with you."

The big man shrugged. "You don't cooperate, I break the old man's fingers."

Moira's knees knocked together as all the fight drained from her body. Hurt her grandfather if she didn't cooperate. Who wanted her? Why?

"Don't go with them, Moira," Seamus said.

The gun was pushed against the side of his head.

"Not another word, old man. The boss wants her, and the boss is going to get her."

She stiffened. Only one person wanted her that badly, the son of a bitch.

"Okay then," she snarled and stabbed her finger at the man with the gun. "Let's go. But understand this, if you so much as hurt a hair on my grandfather's head, you'll regret it to your dying day. And I'm not kidding. I wasn't afraid of your boss last night, and I'm not afraid of him now."

Her kidnapper laughed. "Yeah, I'm real scared. Now, let's go."

Shoving a chair out of her way, Moira stomped across the kitchen past both men and stepped into the garden. If Artemis Gray thought he was going to endear himself to her by threatening her, he was dead wrong. By the time she was finished with him, he'd be sorry he ever met her.

"Don't call the cops, old man, not if you want to see her alive again."

With those words, the both men turned and followed Moira out of the house.

Seamus whirled his wheelchair and headed for the front foyer. There on the hall table he found the spare key where Moira had left it. Next to it lay the business card he'd noticed before he'd gone to bed the last night. The black card with silver ink. It had to be Artemis Gray's home phone number. Moira thought he was behind her kidnapping, but everything Seamus knew about werewolves told him that Artemis would just come get her himself, not send lackeys.

He grabbed the phone and punched in the number. It only rang twice.

"Moira?"

"No. This is her grandfather. And if you're not the one who just had her kidnapped, she's in danger."

A small bit of the worry wrapped around Seamus's heart eased when the other end of the line went dead. Only a fool would lay his hands on the mate of a werewolf.

Exactly twenty-eight minutes later, the front door exploded open. Plaster splattered to the floor as the door crashed into the wall and stuck there. The doorknob was buried completely into the drywall.

Seamus wheeled his chair back out of the way as the man he presumed to be Artemis Gray stalked into the foyer.

"Where?" he barked. The black look on Artemis's face didn't bode well for the men who'd taken Moira.

"The kitchen. They came through the garden. Probably had a car waiting."

"I'll find her, " he snarled and stalked past Seamus. A younger version of Artemis followed him. Both men disappeared through the kitchen door. Seamus heard glass crunch, then all was silent.

"You don't seem too upset for a man whose granddaughter has just been kidnapped."

Seamus turned his attention back to the door and smiled at the pretty girl who stood there. "Come into my house and be welcome. I'm Seamus O'Brien, and you are?"

She jerked the door free of the wall and said, "Sorry for my father's lack of manners. I'm Belle. Now, why aren't you worried."

Seamus nodded to the hole in the wall. "Whoever took Moira wants her alive, so she'll be fine. With as angry as your father is, I'd worry more about the two fools who took her, if I were inclined to worry about them."

Belle nodded. "That's why Brendan went with him, damage control. When father finds out who the mastermind behind this abduction is, someone will have to keep him from killing the idiot."

"Brendan's your brother?"

"Yes."

"Well then, I've nothing to worry about, do I?" Seamus said with a grin.

Belle stared into the white-haired man's sparkling blue eyes. He had a sharp mind in his crippled body, one that saw far more than most people probably realized.

"Who do you think is behind the kidnapping?"

Seamus shrugged. "Why, that harridan Sylvia James. Without Moira, James Parfumes is nothing. When old Mr.

James died, Sylvia fired any chemist who'd been there long enough to call her Sylvia. Their expertise went with them."

Belle grinned. "And I'll just bet you're in the habit of calling Ms. James 'Sylvia' to her face."

Seamus grinned back. "She was a nasty child. Always putting her nose where it didn't belong whenever her father brought her to the lab. More than once, I told him that he should take her over his knee and give her the spanking she deserved. He never took my advice."

Planting her hands on her hips, Belle chuckled and cocked her head to the side. Her nostrils flared as she inhaled. "I think there's more to you than meets the eye, Seamus O'Brien."

Seamus's eyes sparkled even more brightly as he leaned forward and took her hand. "Come in Belle Gray and make yourself at home. There's coffee ready, or I can brew you some fine tea if you'd like. Then I'll tell you the story of a small village in the wilds of northern Wales where some of the finest flowery salves and tinctures were brewed while the wolves bayed at the moon."

Chapter Eight

Ʂ

"Ouch, you stupid ass. You pulled my hair," Moira snapped as the smelly hood was pulled from her head.

"You have a pretty smart mouth, bitch," Gimpy—as Moira now thought of him since he walked with a limp—said. "I'd shut it before I got hurt if I was you.

Moira lifted her hands straight out before her. "You can untie me now. We both know your boss doesn't want me hurt, so you can cut out the threatening act."

"Untie her," the other kidnapper said. "It's not like she'll be able to get away with the both of us in here."

Moira flinched mentally when the man in front of her pulled a switchblade out of his pocket and flicked it open, but she held her hands perfectly still as he sawed through the clothesline he'd used to tie her wrists together.

"There. Now go sit over on that couch until we tell you to move."

She crossed her arms over her chest and snapped. "I don't want to."

"I've had enough of your fucking bullshit, bitch." Reaching out, he grabbed Moira by the front of her robe, lifted her, and threw her across the room onto the dumpy, moth-eaten sofa.

She landed in a heap, her silk robe and nightgown sliding up her thighs.

"She got really nice legs," blue ski mask said.

Moira jerked the gown and robe down over her thighs. "You touch me and you won't be working for Artemis much longer."

"Don't know no Artemis, bitch," Gimpy said with a gap-toothed smile.

"Can we play a little?" blue ski masked asked his companion.

Moira's anger was quickly replaced with fear as their eyes roamed up and down her body. Pulling her legs up onto the couch, she covered them with her robe. Grasping the edges, she held them together under her chin. They didn't know Artemis? Then who'd kidnapped her?

"Obviously your boss wants me in one piece," Moira stated, failing to keep the quaver out of her voice.

"We ain't supposed to hurt her," Gimpy said in a low voice. "We best leave her alone. Don't want to lose any money 'cause she's hurt. You can go fuck that whore you like after we get paid."

Swallowing, Moira stiffened her body to keep from shaking. Even though Gimpy had said no, blue ski mask glanced furtively her way. After a quick glance to see if Gimpy was watching, he pursed his lips and blew a kiss to her. Moira wasn't able to control her trembling after that. She blinked, but a few tears escaped to roll down her cheeks. As long as she'd thought Artemis had kidnapped her, she knew she wasn't in any danger. She was absolutely sure to the depths of her soul that he wouldn't hurt her. But if Artemis wasn't involved, who was? And why had she been kidnapped in the first place?

Huddling into a corner of the old, worn sofa, she fought against the fear that threatened to overwhelm her.

"How much longer we gonna sit here?" complained blue ski mask. "I'm hungry. And this mask itches. How come I can't take it off?"

"Because," Gimpy said as he shuffled his cards for another game of solitaire, "she ain't supposed to know who we are."

"She already don't know who we are."

"And it's gonna stay that way. Now quit bitching."

Before blue ski mask could answer, the door flew open. It slammed against the wall and rebounded only to be wrenched from its hinges and thrown into the room.

Artemis stepped into the room. Nostrils flaring, his gaze darted about the room until it came to rest on Moira. For a second, the steely look in his eyes softened. "Moira, are you all right?"

Heart in her throat, she nodded. Fool. What did he think he was doing. These guys had guns.

Any hint of softness disappeared from Artemis's eyes as he turned his attention back to the two men who'd jumped to their feet when he'd entered the room.

Grinning, Gimpy cracked his knuckles. "You looking for something, old man?"

Blue ski mask lumbered over to stand next to his buddy.

Moira jumped to her feet. "Artemis, get out of here and call the police. They have guns."

He ignored her.

Brendan's voice drifted into the room from behind his father. "Want any help, Dad?"

Artemis's voice was hard. "No. They're mine."

Brendan stepped into the room, crossed his arms over his chest, and leaned back against the wall. "Well, if you need any help, just say so."

"Brendan," Moira begged, "please get some help."

"I don't need any help, Moira," Artemis snarled through clenched teeth. Then he sprang.

Moira gasped. One instant Artemis was standing just inside the door. A second later, he was burying his fist in Gimpy's stomach. As the big man doubled over, Artemis swung around and planted his foot in blue ski mask's crotch. Screaming in agony, he collapsed.

The sound of a gunshot reverberated through the room. Moira screamed as Artemis fell to the floor.

An evil grin spread across Gimpy's face. Then Artemis rolled, leaped to his feet, and buried his left fist in Gimpy's stomach. As the big man doubled over again, a hard uppercut from Artemis snapped his head back. Artemis followed the uppercut with a fist squarely into Gimpy's nose. Cartilage crunched as it flattened. The revolver skittered across the floor as Gimpy slumped unconscious to the floor next to his still moaning and writhing companion.

Panting, his hands still fisted, Artemis turned to Moira. The look in his eyes caused her to take a step back.

"Well, I can tell when I'm not wanted," Brendan said in a cheerful voice. "I'll just clean up the mess." Grabbing both men by their shirt collars, he dragged them from the room.

Kicking the man at his feet out of his way, Artemis stalked across the room towards Moira. "Mine," he growled when he reached her. Pulling her into his arms, he covered her mouth with a hard, demanding kiss.

Moira shivered in his arms and opened her mouth to his stabbing tongue. Artemis's teeth clashed against hers as his kiss not only dominated but also drew forth a feral response from her soul Moira never realized existed. She wrapped her arms around his waist and plastered her body against his.

"Mine," he growled again when he finally stopped ravaging her mouth.

Allowing her head to drop back, Moira stared into Artemis's stormy gaze. A wild beast stared back at her, but instead of being frightened, she was excited. Heat jolted through her body. Her nipples hardened as her breasts swelled. Moisture seeped into her panties. She wanted this man. She needed him. "Yours," she moaned as a lust she'd never before experienced surged though her body.

He pushed her back towards the couch and growled, "Submit."

"Yes," Moira answered. She felt like putty in his hands as he spun her around and pushed her onto her knees on the couch. She dropped her arms, and her silk robe seemed to flow from her body as Artemis pulled it off of her shoulders. Then he ripped her nightgown down the back. It fell from her body to drape across the lumpy cushions beneath her. Moira leaned forwards against the back of the couch and opened herself fully to Artemis.

His hands stroking Moira's back and ass, Artemis struggled to subdue the rage that still surged through his veins. They had taken his mate! He should have ripped out their throats and let their hot blood run down his throat. Should have pounded them until their bones broke, and they howled in agony. His hands tightened on Moira's ass.

She moaned and spread her legs wider.

Artemis shuddered as the spicy, earthy aroma of Moira's heat drifted to his nostrils. Between her hot scent and the triumph throbbing in his veins, Artemis's desire to have all acknowledge his Alpha status dominated his mind and body. The werewolf in him seized control. He had fought and won his mate. What's more Moira, in full heat, kneeled submissively before him, her body arched and spread, waiting for his cock.

She sobbed and pushed back against his fingers when he slid them down the crack in her ass to her dripping slit. He thrust first two, then three fingers into her.

"Please, Artemis. I need you inside of me."

Artemis's cock jerked against the confines of his jeans. Ripping them open, he shoved them down over his hips, toed his loafers off, and kicked his jeans away. He ripped his shirt off his chest. He leaned closer to her and inhaled.

Moira's irresistible fragrance wrapped itself around him. He had to taste her.

Only Artemis's firm grip on her hips kept Moira from leaping over the back of the couch when he lapped the moisture from the inside of her thighs. Arching her back, she spread her legs wider as his tongue lapped first one thigh then the other. Moaning, she arched more, trying to force his mouth and tongue where she wanted them.

"Please, Artemis."

The lapping stopped. The sensitive skin of her clit tingled and ached.

Artemis blew, and warm air swirled between her legs. "What do you want?"

"Your mouth, your tongue, your teeth."

His answer was to stab his tongue into her as deeply as he could.

She ground her crotch into his face as he lapped and suckled. When he gently nipped her clit, she screamed and clamped her thighs against his face. Once more, and she would come.

Artemis grabbed her thighs and spread them, pulling his magic tongue from her body.

Moira struggled against him. Her body was so hot, so achy with the need to explode. He couldn't stop now. She pushed herself away from the back of the couch and tried to turn. "No, Artemis. Don't stop. I need to come. Now!"

He gripped the back of her neck with one hand. "No! Submit!"

For a few seconds, the urge to rebel reared its head. Moira tensed her muscles, ready to struggle against his hold.

"Mine," he snarled again. "Submit." He slid his cock between her thighs and rubbed it against her slippery lips.

Sexual heat erupted outward from Moira's groin, and the urge to have a steel-hard cock plunged into her dissolved any thoughts of rebellion.

"Yours," she gasped again.

Artemis reached between her thighs and spread her slippery lips. Then, with one powerful thrust that drove her forward until her upper torso was hanging over the back of the sofa, he rammed his cock into her.

Panting, Moira braced her hands against the window sill behind the couch and thrust her hips back against Artemis. After a few awkward bucks, she caught the rhythm of his thrusts. Never had anything felt so good!

"Oh, God, yes!" she moaned when Artemis leaned over her back and nipped her neck.

When he clamped his teeth down on her shoulder and began to pump harder, she yelped with pleasure.

Draped over her back, the werewolf in Artemis held Moira submissive to his pleasure, to the necessity that he mate and spread his seed to insure offspring with his genes would survive into another generation.

The fact that she was enjoying what he was doing as much as he did delighted the human half of his soul.

As her slick internal muscles tightened around his cock, Artemis released her shoulder, nipped her, and bit down again. He reached underneath her and kneaded her breast. Then he pinched her nipple. She moaned, and her entire body shuddered. The muscles trying to milk his cock flexed and tightened. He growled and thrust harder. The werewolf half of him wanted to release his seed. His human half wanted to prolong the pleasure, but he wasn't going to be able to last much longer.

Releasing Moira's shoulder, Artemis lifted himself off of her back and arched. Bracing against her ass, he thrust as deeply as he could and rotated his hips.

Beneath him, Moira stiffened.

A low, keening howl escaped her throat as the muscles around his cock contracted one final time, sucked him deeper, then began to vibrate.

Artemis threw back his head and howled as hot come surged through his cock and exploded into Moira's hot, sopping, shuddering body.

Gasping for breath, Moira wiped the tears from her cheeks.

Artemis lay on her back pressing small kisses against her shoulder blades, his cock still embedded inside of her.

Moira shifted, and the crisp hairs on his legs rasped against the tender skin of her inner thighs.

When Artemis wiggled his hips, she sighed with pleasure. "Hmmmm. Can we do that again?"

Chuckling, Artemis lifted himself off her back and slid his cock out of her body. "If you don't mind, next time we make love, I'd like it to be in a bed."

Turning, Moira sank down onto what remained of her nightgown. "And if you don't mind, I'd like to take my clothes off instead of having you rip them off."

Grinning, Artemis shook his head. "I can't make that promise. Hell, I can't even be sure if we'll make it to a bed. You're just too damn sexy."

Moira smiled at the warm feeling that permeated her body. Artemis thought she was sexy.

Before she could say anything, he dropped to one knee.

"You didn't give me an answer last night. Will you marry me, Moira Archer?"

"Oh!" She blinked away the tears that suddenly welled in her eyes. Launching herself off the couch, she threw her arms around his neck. "Yes! Yes, Artemis Gray, I'll marry you."

He kissed her long, tenderly, thoroughly. When he finally lifted his mouth from hers, he said, "You'll accept the transfusion of my blood?"

Blinking, Moira gathered her scattered wits. What was a blood transfusion after all? "Yes."

Artemis grinned. "Good. It will make your pregnancy easier."

Moira's wits were now all firmly where they belonged. "Pregnancy? Now wait a minute, buster. We have to talk about this. I'm the one who has to carry a baby. I'll decide when we have one."

Artemis kissed her nose. "Then you want to have children?"

Moira wrapped her arms around his waist and rubbed her breasts against his chest. The hairs there did such wonderful things to her nipples. "Of course. I just intend to have some input about when we have them."

Artemis chuckled again. "I'll be sure to remember that for the next one."

Moira stopped concentrating on how her nipples were feeling. "What do you mean, the next one."

His smile was gentle. "Moira, love, you're in heat, and I'm a werewolf. You're pregnant."

"But, but..."

"I love you, Moira."

Her hand slid to her stomach. "A baby?"

Artemis hugged her tight against his chest. "Yes, I'm sorry if you're not happy, but I couldn't have stopped if I'd wanted to."

Moira felt her lips twitch into a small smile. Artemis's baby. She glanced up into his face. "It better be a girl. I don't know if I could handle another male as arrogant as you."

A devilish light appeared in his eyes. "I can't predict the sex, love, but I can tell you this. You're having twins."

Epilogue

ᘛ

The pounding on the front door was so loud, Sylvia heard it all the way back in her drawing room. "Excuse me," she said in a perturbed tone to the other three women gossiping over tea.

Rising, she sauntered from the room, closing the door firmly behind her. Once the other women couldn't see her, she allowed the placid mask to slip from her face as she stomped towards her front door. Where was that lazy butler?

The butler was hurrying down the hallway from the kitchen and reached the door just before she did. "I'm sorry, Madam. There was a problem with the grocer."

"I don't give a damn about your problems. You're supposed to be here to open the door. Now open it."

"Yes, Ma'am," he answered through clenched teeth.

As soon as he turned the knob, he was knocked out of the way as the door was shoved open.

Brendan Gray walked in, dragging the two men who'd kidnapped Moira behind him, without their masks. "Yours, I believe," he said as he dropped them at Sylvia's feet.

Speechless, at first, Sylvia quickly regained her composure. "What do you think you're doing? Who are these men? I've never seen them before in my life."

Pulling a small tape recorder from his pocket, Brendan pressed the play button.

The blood drained from Sylvia's face as the two men revealed the entire kidnapping plot.

"You really are a stupid woman, Sylvia," Brendan said as he dropped the recorder back into his pocket. "Now, unless you want this tape delivered to the police, you will pack your bags and move to your house in Florida. And you can forget about James Parfumes. We warned you what would happen if you tried anything stupid. Gray Enterprises is buying up all available stock. At the moment, we own forty-five percent."

"That's not enough for a majority," Sylvia whined.

Brendan smiled. "Not alone. But, according to what I've learned, Moira's grandfather and the other three senior chemists you fired when you assumed control own ten percent of the shares. Somehow, I don't think it will take much to either acquire their shares outright or convince them to vote with us."

"You son of a bitch," Sylvia spit.

Brendan grinned. "You have no idea." Spinning on his heel, he walked out the door.

IN THE HEAT OF THE NIGHT

ഇ

Chapter One

ꕥ

A bead of sweat trickled down Serena's nose, dangled momentarily from the tip, and then splattered onto the musty floor of the den. Groaning, she wiped her forehead on her dirty shirt sleeve in a futile effort to keep more salty perspiration out of her eyes. She inched forward a bit, growling when her knee landed on a particularly sharp rock.

"Damn, Summer, couldn't you have dug out a bigger den?" she grumbled. "You're lucky I'm not claustrophobic."

The wolf simply whimpered as her third cub was born.

Serena sucked in dust with the stale air, coughed, then mumbled under her breath. A protruding root gouged her hip. Shifting, she tried to find a more comfortable position. She'd been belly down in Summer's burrow for the last six hours, and her muscles, the ones she could still feel, were screaming for movement. The wolf whined again and gave the young woman's cheek a wet swipe with her tongue. Then the new mother turned to her whimpering babies.

Serena waited for a few moments more to make sure all three pups were nursing well. After a last caress for their mother's head, she pushed herself backwards and wiggled out of the den, a process that took twenty minutes. Once outside, she rested a moment on her hands and knees and gulped fresh, rain-washed air. Groaning as her stiff muscles protested, she pushed herself to her feet. Straightening, she rose on her toes and stretched her arms into the air. Settling back on her feet, she rolled first her neck then her shoulders. Placing her hands on her hips, she arched. Her back cracked. "Ahhhhh."

Once her muscles were looser, Serena looked at the dark gray wolf pacing back and forth in front of the den. Grinning at the nervous father, she said, "Three, Shadow, all of them healthy. And Summer's fine. You can relax now."

After a quick lick on her hand, the wolf stuck his head in the den. His soft whine was followed by his mate's low growl. He backed out so fast he flopped down on his rump.

Laughing at the amazement and confusion on his face, Serena squatted down and placed her arm around his powerful shoulders. "It's not personal, Shadow. She's tired and needs to rest. You should do the same. I'll see you all tomorrow."

Whining, the wolf lay down, nose pointed towards the den.

Goosebumps tickled Serena's arms when a fresh, spring breeze wrapped itself around her. Shivering, she rubbed her arms and sank onto a log that lay near the den. Smiling, she inhaled more fresh air and closed her eyes. Gods, how she loved her job. She'd really lucked out meeting the guy in town who'd just quit working here. The preserve had been too isolated, he'd complained. Not enough social life. Well, isolation and no social life suited her just fine, so she'd hitched a ride to the preserve's entrance and hiked down the mile long dirt road to the main buildings to find the preserve's owner Dr. Kearnan Gray at his wit's end. He was leaving for Canada and had no one to care for the two wolves already on the preserve.

Dr. Gray had been leery about hiring her, she'd only been nineteen at the time, but he'd been in a bind. After a quick test to see what she knew about wolves and an even quicker introduction to the mated pair already on the preserve to see how they reacted to her, Dr. Gray had hired her and left within the hour. When he'd returned a week later with two more wolves, he'd hired her permanently. She'd been here ever since.

Serena chuckled mentally. Before he left, Dr. Gray had introduced her to Rajah and Beryl to gauge her reactions to the wolves. Rajah, especially, was intimidating, quite large with only one eye and an ugly scar where his other eye should be. Much to Dr. Gray's surprise, Rajah had butted his head against her hand and demanded a pat. Dr. Gray had been even more surprised by her reaction. She'd gotten down on her knees and hugged the wolf.

Serena chuckled to herself again. As if she and the wolves would ever have any trouble getting along.

Rolling her shoulders some more, Serena thought back to that first meeting with Kearnan Gray. It had been—uncanny. When she'd gotten close enough to stick out her hand and introduce herself, a startled look had appeared in his eyes and his nostrils had flared, almost as if he were taking in her scent. An intense look had appeared on his face, and he'd seemed ready to say something. But then, Rajah had whined, and Gray's attention had returned to the wolf.

Serena shivered. That first meeting had left her with an eerie feeling. There was something about Kearnan Gray, something she just couldn't put her finger on, but she'd shrugged it off as nervousness on her part about getting the job. After Dr. Gray had returned from Canada and she'd gotten to know him better, gotten to see how he cared for the wolves, her interest in him had blossomed. Sometimes she'd caught him staring at her with a puzzled or speculative look on his face, but he always pulled his gaze away. And she certainly didn't want him interested in her, did she?

A cloud of gnats descended on Serena and jolted her from her memories. She waved her arms impotently for a minute then rose to her feet. Her forehead itched. When she reached up to scratch it, bits of caked mud dribbled into her hand. She lifted her hand to rub the back on her neck and got a whiff of her own stench.

"Gods, but I need a shower," she muttered.

Serena wiped her dirty hands on her butt. What was a little more dirt on her jeans anyway? She tucked a loose strand of her black hair back behind her ears and pulled two twigs from what was left of her French braid. When she rubbed her cheek, more dirt fell onto her fingers. She looked back at the gray wolf. "I'm really a mess, aren't I, Shadow?"

He ignored her.

After one last grin for the worried father, Serena grabbed the small bag of supplies she'd brought with her, turned, and hiked through the pathless forest. Shadow and Summer's enclosure was roughly five square miles, and she was grateful Summer had decided the perfect place for her den was so close to the gate. It saved a lot of walking. The fact that it was after dark didn't bother her. *She* had no trouble seeing in the dark. Besides, the moon was almost full. She had all the light she needed to see where she was going.

Once outside the gate, Serena dusted off her behind as best she could then slid into the golf cart, a smile curving her lips. Considering this was Summer's first litter, the birthing had gone very well. Now, once she got all the details entered in the log, she could go to her snug, little cabin for some much needed sleep. Tired but happy, she headed back to the preserve's main buildings. Three more beautiful wolf pups had entered the world, and, here on the private preserve, they were safe from humans who didn't understand them. Life didn't get any better than this.

Stopping in front of the sanctuary's clinic, Serena slid out of the cart and gathered up her equipment. Pushing open the door, she flipped the light switch and headed for her office. She was busy recording the information about the new wolf pups when a slight noise caught her attention. Her nostrils flared as the scent of spicy cologne wafted into the room. Before she could stop herself, she inhaled deeply. The woodsy aroma invaded her senses, and she shuddered. Damn, she hadn't wanted to see *him* tonight. Thank all the gods she was leaving right away in the morning. This was not a good time to be fantasizing about her boss.

The office door opened. Glancing up, Serena looked into the face of Dr. Kearnan Gray . She remained perfectly still, but her senses snapped to full alert. Something about him was different. His scent had changed; he smelled—eager. Yes, that's what was different, the anticipation. Why? What did he want? Was that a question in his eyes? Swallowing nervously, she jerked her eyes back to her ledger.

She felt rather than saw him lean against the doorjamb. Glancing up from beneath her eyelashes, Serena focused on the man who, lately, spent entirely too much time in her dreams.

Barely six feet tall, lithe and lean rather than bulky with muscles, Kearnan Gray's form still seemed to fill the doorway.

A small smile tickled the corners of his mouth as he stared at her.

Serena avoided eye contact and let her gaze wander down his body. Gods help her, but she never got tired of looking at him.

Wide shoulders, a broad chest, but not too broad, her boss was definitely not barrel chested. No, he was not bulky with muscles but rather muscular with a well-toned body. His stomach was flat and his hips slim.

Deliberately skipping over the bulge between his thighs, Serena's gaze continued to drift down his body. Concentrating on that most interesting part of his anatomy would fluster her even more. Instead, she admired how his jeans clung to his muscular thighs.

Serena sighed mentally. Too bad he didn't turn around. He had a great ass. More than once she'd watched his taut buttocks flexing underneath tight fitting jeans as she climbed hills behind him.

His voice was amused. "Like what you see?"

Jerking her eyes back to the book in front of her, Serena pretended interest in her ledger, but she didn't see a word written there. Sighing she closed her eyes. She didn't need to have them open to see his face. She had every detail memorized.

Her boss was too good-looking for his own good. Rather, her own good. Some women might be put off by the sharp angles of his face and prematurely gray, no—silvery-gray, hair—but she wasn't. As far as she was concerned, his hair was perfect. So were his lips, not too thin, not too full, and the bump on his nose from when he broke it last winter was sexy. Not even that small scar high on his left cheek marred his good looks.

But it was Kearnan Gray's eyes that fascinated Serena more than any other feature on his face, his gray eyes. Eyes that were the color of a soft gray mist on a summer day when he was happy, the color of dark, stormy gray of thunderclouds when he was puzzled or unhappy, or the hard iron gray color of tempered steel when he was angry. What color gray would they be when he was lost in passion?

Lost in passion? Down, girl, Serena admonished herself as she struggled to fill in the information about the birth and ignore her boss at the same time. Get your mind back on your business—the wolf cubs. *Maybe it would be better if I forget about sleeping and leave as soon as I get finished here. Dr. Gray is becoming entirely too enticing, especially with the full moon tomorrow night. Besides, there's no way anything but a business relationship between the two of us will ever work. Every one of my relationships sucked.*

Gray's husky voice pulled her back to the present. "Everything went well?"

She misspelled a word.

"Yes," she answered without looking up. "Three new pups, two males, one female, all healthy."

"Great." He stepped further into the small room, and Serena had to force herself not to shiver with anticipation. He was so—masculine, and tonight was not a good time for her to be anywhere near him. Three steps inside the door, he stopped.

Her stomach lurched and she swallowed. Did he sense how nervous he made her? How tense? How horny? *Get a hold of yourself, Serena. It's not full moon yet, thank God.* She sighed with relief at that thought. He would not be amused if she attacked him.

Clasping his hands behind his back, he smiled at her, white teeth gleaming. "When you finish here, I'd like you to come up to the house. I have a new breeding program I'd like to discuss."

She glanced down at her watch. "Could it wait until tomorrow? It's almost 9:30, and I've been up since three A.M. I could really use some sleep." She glanced up.

His smile was amused. "But you're leaving early in the morning. The long weekend you requested, remember? You won't have time to talk then. So, I'm afraid I really must insist since I'll be otherwise engaged for the next week. Tonight is the only time I have to talk to you."

Tensing slightly, Serena didn't try to hide the annoyance in her voice. " I'll be up as soon as I finish this entry."

Still smiling, he nodded. "Good. I'll see you in a few minutes." Pivoting, he sauntered out of the building. The enticing scent of his cologne remained behind.

Serena glared at the empty doorway. Damn! Damn! Damn! She did not need this hassle tonight. And why did he always wear that freaking cologne? He smelled good enough to eat. How was she supposed to keep her mind on her work when he smelled that good?

Groaning, Serena laid her pen down and stared at the now empty doorway. Why did he have to show up tonight of all nights? She needed to sleep a little, and then she had to get out of here. The full moon was tomorrow night. With a sigh she leaned back in her chair and stared at the empty doorway. He was so handsome, so appealing, so sexy! It wasn't fair! She was finally attracted to a male, but he was completely unsuitable. Why couldn't he be like her?

Serena's lips twitched, and she sniffed sardonically to herself. Yeah, just what this world needed, more werewolves running around.

With a muttered oath, she wrenched her thoughts back to the new wolf pups. They were her first priority. Her fantasy life could wait until later. Besides, a man like Kearnan Gray , even if he did love wolves, would never be interested in someone like her, someone he would consider a freak or monster. He'd run screaming if he knew the truth.

After finishing the entry, Serena put the ledger back on the shelf. Yawning once—she really needed to get some sleep—she lifted her arms over her head and stretched. The sudden, aching stab in her groin made her gasp, and she dropped her hand to the apex of her thighs and rubbed herself. An expectant shiver raced up her spine to battle the dismay in her mind. It was starting already. Damn! Maybe she should forget about sleeping and get away from here while she could.

Maybe it was time she left altogether. She'd been here longer than she'd stayed in one place since she ran away from her pack. Staying in one place this long would make it easier for Alex to find her.

"But it's been over three years," Serena mumbled to the empty room. "Surely if Alex were still looking for me, he'd have found me. He's not stupid. He must have finally accepted that I won't mate him."

A twitching stab shot through her groin. "Oh gods, not now!"

Leaning back against the desk, Serena jerked the buttons on her jeans open and shoved her hand down her pants. When her fingers brushed her tender lips, her hips bucked involuntarily. Even as she spread her legs farther apart, she breathed a sigh of relief. She wasn't swollen yet. There was still time for her to get away before her yearly wolf heat manifested itself. Bad enough the werewolf in her made her hornier at her human fertile time. The yearly wolf heat was worse, and this year it coincided with a full moon. There were only three ways to satisfy the urges that bombarded her body during heat: the hard, almost violent 'heat' sex between two werewolves, the hot blood that pumped from the severed jugular of captured prey after a grueling, exhausting hunt, or holding her wolf shape and finding a male wolf to mate with her.

Tomorrow night Serena would hunt and sate the lust in her soul with hot, rich blood. Mating with a wolf was out of the question. All the males on the preserve were mated; and, while in her case the females would bow to Serena's extenuating circumstances, she was still uncomfortable taking other female's mates.

Serena grimaced. No way would she ever use one of the male wolves again, even if the female wolves brushed off her apprehension as a ridiculous human morality.

They knew she didn't want to take their mates, Beryl had explained. Serena was in pain. Using one of the males to relieve that pain was only common sense.

Serena shook her head. The wolves may view human moralities as peculiar and strange, but she *was* human. Using a mated wolf to ease herself was like sleeping with another woman's husband. She simply couldn't do it.

Nor were there any male werewolves around to satisfy her. Even if one magically appeared, there was no way she'd put herself in position to be dominated by one. They were just too damn possessive, especially the Alphas. She'd learned her lesson with Alex. Have sex with them once, and they thought they owned you.

Another lancet of heat speared her. Moaning, Serena braced her other hand on the edge of the desk and arched her back. Her fingers became wetter as she caressed herself, paying special attention to her aching nub hidden between her slick lips. Throwing back her head, she visualized her boss, naked, his cock thick and long. In her mind, he grabbed her hips and slid that hard, hard cock into her, thrusting and swiveling as he pounded against her.

Serena jerked then began to pump, matching the rhythm of her stroking fingers. Tingling aches danced around her nipples, nipples she knew were distended and aching. But she didn't have time. She rubbed harder.

Once, twice, there, the third caress pushed her over the edge, and she shuddered to her climax. Panting, she pulled her hand from her pants, turned and braced both hands on her desk. Not the most earth shattering climax she'd ever given herself, but it would do for now. Surely, her boss wouldn't keep her more than half an hour at the most. She could function normally that long.

Straightening, she buttoned her jeans. Flipping off the light switch, she left her office, stopping only long enough to wash her hands and face in the clinic's sink. One quick glance around the room told her everything was in place. With a sigh, she strode to the door. She'd best get up to the house. The sooner she got there, the sooner Dr. Gray would be done explaining his new breeding program, and the sooner she could leave.

Chapter Two

Hands clasped behind his back, Dr. Kearnan Gray stared out the window at the almost full moon. One more night and Serena Wilde would get the surprise of her life.

A picture of Serena the first time he'd seen her appeared in his mind. Wearing faded blue jeans and an old flannel shirt with a bright orange backpack hanging from her shoulders, she stomped into the clinic and informed him she was here for the job taking care of wolves. She'd had no resume, no references, no qualifications for the job that he could see. She'd looked all of sixteen. But, he was leaving for Canada in half an hour, Jeff Miller had quit not four hours earlier, and Carl Jenkins, his other assistant had been called home because his mother had fallen and broken her leg. Kearnan had been in a jam, and he'd been willing to hire anyone at that point—within reason. If the wolves liked her, he'd hire Serena Wilde.

Motioning her to follow him, he'd taken her to meet his wolves, without the benefit of a chainlink fence between them. Once she met Rajah, he'd know what she was made of.

Inside the enclosure, Serena had surprised the hell out of him. Showing no fear, she had squatted down and thrown her arms around Rajah's neck. The scarred wolf had licked her face and had wagged his tail like a common dog.

Still shocked by the wolf's reaction to her, Kearnan had let his gaze slip down her back to where her tee-shirt had pulled free of her jeans. He'd had a clear view of a wide expanse of the smooth skin—and the tattoo in the small of her back. He recognized the purple flowers intertwined with green leaves immediately, aconite—wolfsbane.

Then the wind had shifted and carried her scent to him as she stuck out her hand to shake his, and he'd felt as if someone buried a fist in his stomach. Serena had smelled of sweat, woman, and aconite—wolfsbane. She had aconite flowers tattooed on her back. It was an ingredient in the perfume she wore. Why? Did she just like the way it smelled or was there a deeper meaning. If Rajah's growl at the car that arrived to take him to the municipal airport hadn't distracted him at that moment, he would have asked her.

Now, Kearnan was glad he hadn't. It had given him time to think about his past and decide what he wanted to do with his future, something that had taken almost three years, three years taking extra care that Serena wasn't put into a position where her true identity was revealed—nor his. But he was sure now. His future included Serena. All he had to do was convince her.

A moan from across the room drew his attention. Turning, he stepped to his desk and sat down. Leaning back in his chair, Kearnan steepled his fingers beneath his chin and watched the television monitor. Since the theft of some medical supplies, he'd had cameras installed in all the buildings, something his employees didn't know. He'd caught his thief. He'd also acquired some very interesting footage of Serena Wilde. As he watched, her fingers dipped into her crotch, and she began to stroke herself. He ignored the erection that strained the front of his jeans as her hips began to pump rhythmically.

Kearnan pursed his lips, surprised that she'd had to masturbate before she met with him. His calculations of her cycle must be slightly off. If Summer hadn't taken so long to birth her pups, Serena would probably be gone by now. He closed his eyes and mentally thanked the new mother wolf. Without her, Serena would have slipped away again.

Another low moan from the monitor pulled Kearnan from his musings. With one last thrust of her hips, Serena climaxed. Leaning forward, he turned the monitor off. Taking a deep breath, he gathered his considerable will and forced his erection to relax. It wouldn't do to have her walk in and see how much he wanted her—not yet anyway. Given her past history, she'd bolt right back out the door. He couldn't wait another year for the time to be right. Tomorrow he would begin to help her understand her sexuality and the pleasures she was missing. She needed a real man to teach her, and he was more than willing to be the one. Then, tomorrow night when the moon was full…

A few minutes later, a sharp rap sounded on his front door. "Come in, Serena, it's open," he called.

He smiled. Considering what she'd just been doing, she hadn't wasted any time getting here.

Warily, Serena entered her boss's foyer and turned right towards the office. Her heightened sense of smell picked up the spicy scent of his cologne, and her nipples puckered. With a groan, she stopped and braced her hand against the wall.

"Are you all right?"

He sounded worried as he stepped out of his office.

Taking a deep breath she pushed away from the wall and forced herself to walk past him into his office. She would get through this. She purposely made her voice grumpy. "I'm just tired. Are you sure you need to talk to me tonight?"

He stood aside so she could precede him into the room. "Yes, it is. I'm sorry. Sit down, please. Would you like some coffee?"

Serena eased herself in the closest chair. "I don't want to stay awake."

His grin was sexy. "How about some herbal tea? It's already brewed."

Serena yanked her gaze away from his face and closed her eyes. The warm, comforting aroma of chamomile and orange swirled lazily around the room and mixed with the crisp smell of burning wood from the fire place. *Herbal tea. Yes.*

That would help, and I need to humor him. The sooner I can find out what he wants, the sooner I can get out of here. "Tea will be fine."

His back to her, Gray busied himself with the tea.

Serena shifted in her seat. She slid back and crossed her legs. Then she uncrossed her legs and pushed forward to the edge of the chair. She glared at her boss's back. What was taking him so long? Why was he farting around with the tea? "Could you please hurry up, Dr. Gray. I'm really tired. I don't really need any tea."

"It's finished." He returned to her side and handed her a mug, his fingers brushing against hers.

Heat surged through her fingers straight to her nipples.

Hot tea sloshed onto her fingers as she jerked her hand away.

"Damn it!" She grabbed the mug in her other hand, stuck her fingers in her mouth, and sucked the hot liquid from them.

When she looked back up, her boss was watching her fingers slide out of her mouth, his silver eyes sparkling with golden speckles.

Dropping her hand to the arm of the chair, she gulped some tea. "This is very good."

He smiled a slow smile that sent a shiver dancing up Serena's spine. "Thank you. It's a special blend."

Serena gulped more tea. Warmth spread outward from her stomach. "Whose breeding program do you want to change?"

His voice was low, compelling, and—eager? "Finish your tea, Serena."

"Fine." She chugged the rest of the tea, wincing as the almost too hot liquid flowed down her throat. She held out the mug. "Here, I'm finished. Now, will you please explain this new breeding program?"

As he took the mug, his fingers brushed hers again. He stared at her with those silvery gold eyes.

Another shiver had her nipples tightening almost painfully.

"Do you feel better now?'

Her temper flared. "Better? I've been belly down in a wolf den for over ten hours, and you ask if I feel better? I'm tired, damn it. I need sleep. Will you stop asking stupid questions and tell me why you wanted to see me!"

Satisfaction and, was that anticipation, appeared on his face. "I've never seen your temper before this."

Oh shit. Serena closed her eyes and swallowed. *I just told off my boss.* She leaned her head back against the chair. Gods, but she was tired. Her body relaxed as a gentle lethargy seeped through her bloodstream. The warm, comforting scents permeating the room embraced her. The crackling sounds of the fire faded.

"Miss Wilde? Serena?"

Serena opened her eyes.

Hands braced on the arms of the chair, Kearnan Gray was bending over her.

Gods, he was handsome. This close, the gold speckles in his eyes seemed to completely cover the silver.

His eyes are as golden as the wolves' eyes.

Soft, silvery hair fell onto his forehead, and she reached up to brush it away.

His nostrils flared. "What do you want from me, Serena?" he asked in a husky voice.

His words penetrated.

"Oh!" She jerked her hand back and struggled to push herself into an upright position. "I'm sorry. I'm so tired, I guess I started to drift off."

He straightened but didn't move away.

Serena shook her head and opened her eyes wider. Gods, she'd almost fallen asleep in her boss's office! Groggily, her mind grasped at her reason for being here. "What—what was it you want to talk to me about?"

He stared down at her, a strange smile on his face. "A new breeding program."

She yawned then frowned. "All the wolves are paired. You know they mate for life. Who's program do you want to change?"

Crossing his arms over his chest, Kearnan leaned back against his desk.

Serena was holding herself upright by tightly clasping both arms of the chair. The long hours she'd spent in the wolf's burrow had had a definite effect on her appearance, but she was still, even with twigs in her hair, the most beautiful woman he'd ever seen.

Long strands of thick black hair that had escaped from her braid caressed her cheeks and neck. Thick black lashes brushed her cheeks every time her eyes drifted shut, eyes that were as blue as the sky on a clear day. Her Native American blood was evident in her high cheekbones and wonderfully caramel-colored complexion. Her lips were parted slightly, full red lips that were meant to be kissed. Her nose was crooked, but he didn't care. That slight imperfection only made Serena more beautiful to him.

A streak of dirt meandered down across her neck and disappeared beneath her collar only to reveal itself again in the open vee of her shirt. Kearnan licked his lips as his glance followed the line of dirt lovingly curled over the upper part of her plump breast to disappear into her shadowed cleavage. Her nipples were straining against her thin tee shirt. She wasn't wearing a bra.

Groaning mentally as his cock stirred, he tugged his gaze back to her face. More than anything, he wanted to bury his face between those lush breasts, to fondle and kiss them, to suck her pert nipples into his mouth. What color were they, he often wondered. A ripe rosy pink or warm, cinnamony brown? Soon, he would find out.

Serena's eyelids drooped again. Again she forced them open, unaware of the silent invitation she sent him. She looked so—delectable. He moistened his lips again and shifted as his body responded. If this kept up, he'd take her here and now, and she wasn't ready for him—yet.

"Dr. Gray ," she repeated as she forced her eyes open yet again, "whose breeding program do you want to change?"

"You've been working for me for more than three years now, and you still call me Dr. Gray . My name is Kearnan, say it."

Her forehead wrinkled with concentration and she blinked—once. "Why?"

He cocked an eyebrow. "Why what?" She was almost asleep.

She shook her head, obviously trying to dismiss the lethargy invading her body. "Why should I call you Kearnan?"

"Don't you think we know each other well enough by now?"

Serena shook her head to clear the fog flowing into her brain. What did he say? How long had she been here? She had to get out of here. "No, yes, I don't know. Please, I'm tired. Whose breeding program do you want to talk about—Kearnan?"

Pushing away from his desk, he stepped closer. Her eyes slid down his tapered chest to his crotch. They widened when she saw the huge bulge in the front of his jeans. Slowly, her gaze traveled its length from top to bottom and back up again. She licked her lips then leaned her head back and looked up into his face. When he bent over and braced his hands on the arms of her chair, she pressed herself as far back as she could.

"You smell of woman and passion," he whispered into her ear. He nuzzled her neck.

Goosebumps exploded all over her body. Her nipples ached.

His wet tongue prodded the sensitive spot behind her ear. "Whose breeding program am I changing? Yours."

She bent her neck to give him better access. Gods, she didn't even know that was a sensitive spot.

Then, the meaning of his words sank in, and the exhaustion and strange languor she'd been feeling disappeared from her mind. She jerked her head away from his.

He pulled away and leaned back against his desk.

She gawked at him silently. Then, her chin jerked up. "*My* breeding program! Are you nuts?"

"No. You see, Serena, I know you're a werewolf."

Chapter Three

Panic and adrenaline surged through Serena's veins. *How did he find out? He can't know for sure. It's just a wild guess. Everybody knows werewolves don't exist.* "Werewolf? You're freaking crazy! I'm not going to stay here and listen to asinine accusations." She pushed against the arms of the chair and commanded her body to rise.

Her body disobeyed.

Serena tried to force herself up. Again her body refused her command. Jerking her chin up, she glared at her boss.

Triumph shone in his eyes.

Realization dawned, and she felt the blood drain from her face. "The tea. You've drugged me."

Kearnan tilted his head to the side, and his wolfish smile became tender. "I had no choice. You were going to leave."

"So you drug me to throw preposterous allegations into my face?"

He shook his head. "Not so preposterous. I know the truth about you. It took me a while, but I've discovered your secret."

Desperation crept into Serena's voice. "You're crazy. Werewolves are a myth. They don't exist outside of silly romance novels or Hollywood horror movies."

With a rueful shake of his head, Kearnan returned to her chair and swiveled it around to face the television. "Your stubbornness is one of the things I admire so much about you. You never give up. I have some video for you to watch."

She paled. "Video?"

He chuckled, but his back remained towards her as he pulled a video from the shelf. "You know that I have at least four cameras mounted in every wolf enclosure." He didn't wait for an answer but slid the cassette into the VCR. Then he pulled another chair next to hers and sat down. "Two years ago, a most amazing thing happened in Rajah and Beryl's enclosure. A black, female wolf appeared out of nowhere and mated with Rajah. Even more amazing, Beryl didn't challenge her."

Serena said nothing she watched the huge male wolf mate with the smaller female. When they finished, the strange female melted away into the shadows.

Kearnan fast-forwarded the tape. "Almost exactly one year later, the same female wolf appeared again. This time she chose Shadow, a better choice since he wasn't mated yet. Even so, he didn't act normally. Oh, he participated in the mating enthusiastically enough, as you can see."

Her cheeks warming, Serena silently watched the gray wolf mount the female.

"But when they were finished, she disappeared. What surprised me was that Shadow made no attempt to stop her. He didn't have a mate. He should have tried to keep her with him."

"Dr. Gray , you have footage of an unknown female wolf," Serena interrupted. "How does that justify you accusations?"

"I thought we agreed that you'd call me Kearnan."

She pinched her lips together and stared at him without answering.

Smiling, he leaned over and pushed the eject button. Then he replaced the tape with another one. "Granted, those two tapes prove nothing, but they did capture my interest. After all, you were absent both times that female wolf appeared."

She shook her head emphatically. "So that makes me a werewolf? You've been watching too many horror movies."

"No, sweetheart," he replied gently.

"I am not your sweetheart."

He smiled that wolfish smile again. "You will be."

She snorted and turned her head away.

"Serena, do you remember the rash of thefts we experienced last year?"

Reluctantly, she nodded her head.

"I had video cameras install in all the preserve's buildings. Since I didn't know who the thief was, I didn't tell any of you."

Serena would have spoken but he held up his hand. "I know, too many people employed here for me to install cameras everywhere without someone knowing. Well, I simply waited until you requested one of your long weekends—during a full moon, I might add—and gave everyone else the weekend off. The security company had everything completed in a day and a half, and no one was the wiser."

"So that's how you knew Jerry was the one stealing medical supplies."

"Caught him red-handed so to speak. But, Serena, there are other far more interesting recordings. This one for example."

He pushed the play button on the remote and the blood drained from her face. Those were her moans and gasps, her naked body lying back on the examining table in the clinic. She didn't need to watch. Instead she closed her eyes and relived one of the most frustrating nights of her life.

She leaned against the table waiting for Tim, wondering if she was doing the right thing. They'd been on a few dates, and he'd been the perfect gentleman every time. He was really cute with dimples to die for and a sexy smile, and sooo charming. Tim had seemed so interested in her, encouraging her to talk about herself—not that she told him anything important. And his kisses…Maybe, just maybe, it would work between them. Tonight, full moon, she'd agreed to meet him in the clinic after hours. It had been so long since she'd had sex with a man, and she was more than ready. She was thankful she wasn't in her werewolf heat. She might scare him away.

The soft swish of the door opening caught her attention, and she smiled when Tim appeared. He was good-looking in a rugged sort of way, at five foot eight, not tall but still taller than her own five foot two. He had blond hair and green eyes, but it was his personality that had drawn her to him, out-going, friendly, and most importantly, nonjudgmental. He accepted her for what she was; of course, he didn't know she was a werewolf. If things worked out, maybe, someday …

His grin was infectious. "Hello, babe. Waiting long?"

Smiling, she shook her head. "Not really. I had some paperwork to do. I just finished." She stepped closer to him. The moon was rising. She had urges to be satisfied one way or another.

Grinning, Tim pulled her into his arms and thrust his crotch against her thigh. "You sure about this, babe?"

"Yes." She wrapped her arms around his neck, rubbed her breasts against his chest, and lifted her mouth to his.

His kiss was not drawn out or passion inducing. Instead, he stabbed his tongue into the back of her throat, almost choking her. His hands wrenched her shirt open and yanked it free from her jeans, not caring that buttons popped and the soft cotton ripped. Gagging, Serena tried to pull her mouth from his. Werewolf sex could get rough, but it was pleasurable. Tim just seemed like he was in a hurry.

When her shirt was off, he made short work of her bra. Looking down at her rose tipped breasts, he panted. "I'm so horny, babe. Come on. Don't make me wait."

His hands jerked her jeans open and slipped them and her panties down over her hips. Grasping her waist, he lifted her up onto the table. Her sandals fell to the floor and jeans and panties slipped down over her ankles.

Jerking his own jeans open, Tim freed his cock. After stroking it a few times, he shoved his hand between her legs. "Oh yeah, babe. You're good and juicy."

Serena gasped at his clumsy groping. This wasn't what she expected. Where were the kisses and caresses she read about in all those novels? He wasn't any better than her other two human lovers had been.

"Tim, wait, I…"

But he didn't listen to her. Pulling a condom out of his back pocket, he sheathed himself. Then he pushed her down, grasped her thighs, and pulled her forward until her butt was at the edge of the table. Spreading her legs, he entered her with one thrust, ignoring her surprised cry. His fingers dug into her thighs as he pumped, rising up on his toes to push himself deeper. After only a few minutes, he gasped, groaned, and collapsed on her body.

His hands left her thighs to pinch her nipples. "That was great, babe. We have to do it again," he said as he pushed himself off her, threw the used condom into a waste basket, pushed his cock inside his pants, and pulled up the zipper. "I'll see you tomorrow."

Before Serena could even slide off the table, he was gone.

"No!" A sob escaped her as she crossed her arms over her chest. She tingled and throbbed all over, completely unsatisfied and frustrated. Another in a short list of disappointments. Another human lover had left her unsatisfied. Better the lust for hot blood and the kill. At least it satisfied her. There were lots of deer around the preserve.

Wiping the tears from her cheek, she looked around the room. Then she dipped her fingers between her thighs and rubbed and rubbed and rubbed until her orgasm shuddered through her body. Never again would she depend on a man to satisfy her.

As Serena pulled herself back to the present, her boss turned away from the screen and faced her. Her chin dropped to her chest, and she closed her eyes. Tears trickled down her cheeks. How often had Kearnan watched this tape? Could she feel any more humiliated?

"Just because you have a tape of me and Tim doesn't make me a werewolf. Werewolves don't exist. You need your head examined."

His voice was soft. "Tim was a fool."

Lifting her head, Serena opened her eyes and glared at him. He was watching the television, replaying her sexual encounter. When she glanced at it, she flushed. The camera in the clinic was directly above the examining table, so she looked down on herself, her legs spread wide, hands clutching the table's sides as Tim pounded into her. His white cock, disappearing inside of her then sliding back out, contrasted sharply with her black pubic hair. She glanced back at her employer.

Kearnan didn't look at her. His attention was focused on the television. After he played it through again, he turned his head back to her. "A couple of thrusts, and he was finished. What a fool to think only of his own pleasure when the bounty of your body was spread out before him. If only you had come to me, Serena. I would have made you come over and over before I satisfied my own urges."

He stepped away from the television and returned to her side. His fingers brushed her cheek then trailed down her neck and shoulder to her breast. He caressed it gently, delicately thumbing her aching nipple. "I'd have sucked your nipples, first one then the other, licking and nipping each one until you wept with anticipation. Then, I would have buried my face between your legs and worshiped every fold and crease with my mouth and tongue, nipping and licking your clit until you screamed with your first orgasm. And, I wouldn't have stopped. I would have kept rubbing, and licking, and kissing it until it became so sensitive that you would be able to come with the slightest touch."

"Then, after I'd inhaled your scent and swallowed the unique flavor that is Serena Wilde until my cock was ready to burst, I would have lifted myself over you and spread your legs. As I sucked your sensitive nipple into my mouth, I'd have thrust myself into you as hard and deeply as I could. Both of us would have burned as your hot, juicy muscles clasped and unclasped my aching cock. And, when both of us were ready, I'd have come inside of you while you gushed and shuddered around me. You should have come to me, love. I would have shown you what human sex should be like."

Biting down on her trembling lip to hold back a sob, Serena closed her eyes to hold back her tears as he continued to make love to her with words. Could they? She bit down hard on her lip. No, it was too late. No matter what he said, if he ever saw her when the lust for blood was impossible to resist, he'd run screaming with horror. She had to get away. She opened her eyes.

Kearnan's intense gaze bored into hers. She didn't need to see the erection straining against his jeans to know he was aroused. She smell it.

"Please," she begged. "Let me go. I promise not to press charges." She fought against the drug holding her immobile. If she could only get up; she was faster than he was, much stronger. She could escape if only she could conquer this drug.

Serena's soft words forced themselves past Kearnan's urge to take her there on the chair. Jerking himself away from her, he struggled to control the lust surging through his blood. Not here, not now. It was too early to take her yet.

Turning, he pushed a button on the remote and ejected the tape. After a few deep breaths, he turned his attention back to Serena. "Struggling won't help, sweetheart. I mixed the drug we use to tranquilize the wolves with the tea. You can't get away." He leaned over and tucked a loose curl behind her ear. "I could no sooner let you go than I could cut off my right hand."

She shook her head, slowly. "Kearnan, this is kidnapping."

"Serena, you can't run off into the forest every time you come into heat. You've been lucky so far, but what if someone captures you? Worse, shoots you?"

She ignored him and stared at the wall, refusing to make eye contact.

"It was a full moon that night in the clinic with Tim. But he didn't satisfy you at all. You had to go out to kill to satisfy your lust. When sex with Tim didn't work, you sought blood. I found a dead deer very close to the compound the next day, an obvious wolf kill. But, none of our wolves can get out."

Again she refused to answer.

"I have one last tape for you to watch. Last year when we discovered someone had tried to cut the fence, I turned the northernmost camera in Rajah's enclosure outward. I'm glad I did. Not only did I get enough evidence against the Hadley brothers to give to the sheriff, I got some very interesting footage of you.

Serena stared at the television. Just beyond Rajah's enclosure was a small waterfall with a pool at its base. She often went there to relax. On the screen, she watched as she stripped off her clothes and sank into the pool. It had been a hot day, and she had just wanted to cool off. If it hadn't been for the Hadley brothers…

Kearnan didn't even have to turn up the volume; the noise the two men made crashing through the brush was that audible. Fred and Daryl Hadley were coarse men who had always made her nervous whenever she went into town. The two men seemed to spend most of their time sitting on the porch of the area's only tavern, tossing lewd and raucous comments at any woman who walked by. Even now, knowing they were miles away, their voices still made her shudder. She closed her eyes, but their voices pounded in her ears.

"I tell ya I saw her go this way. Miss Stuck up. She won't be so stuck up with my prick in her ass."

"Ya better be right, Daryl. It's too damn hot to go trampin' through the woods."

Serena shuddered and opened her eyes. They would have raped her. One she could have handled by herself, but not both of them. They were both big, strong men.

"You don't have to worry about them," Kearnan interrupted. "I promise they'll never come near you again."

The Serena in the television bolted from the water. The Hadley brothers were just beyond the mountain laurel. There had been only one way to save herself. She moaned as the Serena on screen vanished in a cloud of black mist to be replaced by a black wolf that disappeared among the hemlock trees on the other side of the clearing.

Kearnan stopped the tape, turned off the television, and turned to her. He cupped her cheek then chuckled as she tried to pull her head away.

Serena fought it the heavy torpor spreading through her veins. She struggled to remain conscious. "What are you going to do with me?"

His thumb caressed her full bottom lip. "I'm going to show you that making love with a man can bring you more pleasure than you dreamed possible."

A tear trickled down her cheek. "No …" Her head dipped, and she jerked it back up. She struggled to keep her eyes open. Her voice was a mere whisper. "Please…"

Kearnan smiled tenderly when her eyes closed for the final time. Bending over, he gathered her into his arms and cuddled her against his chest. She'd sleep the rest of the night. Once morning came, he'd begin his instruction.

Chapter Four

ꟹ

Serena slid her hands up the smooth muscles of Kearnan's back to his shoulders and down along his firm arms. Pressing her bare breasts against his back, she wrapped her arms around his waist, nuzzled his shoulder, and inhaled deeply. As she wrapped both hands around his straining erection, she nibbled his neck…

Serena buried her face deeper in her pillow, paused—and sniffed. Cracking her eyes open, she wrapped her pillow more tightly in her arms and snuggled closer. She frowned and sniffed again. Her pillow didn't smell like this.

Serena's eyes snapped open, and she sprang from the bed. Crouching in the middle of the floor, her gaze darted around the room. Goosebumps raced across her body as the crisp morning air wrapped itself around her. She was naked, and she was cold. More importantly, she was alone.

Rising slowly, she took stock of her surroundings. The room was small; it contained only a small three-drawer dresser and a large bed. Two doors faced each other on opposite walls. The only windows were two skylights in the high ceiling.

"Not as smart as you think you are, Kearnan Gray," Serena said to the empty room. "There isn't a door anywhere on the preserve I can't rip off its hinges. Being a werewolf has its advantages."

Stepping forward, Serena grabbed the doorknob and turned. Locked. Bracing her right hand against the wall, she tightened her grip turned harder.

Ten minutes later she wiped away the sweat beaded on her forehead. The door wouldn't budge. The damn thing must be reinforced. Squeezing the doorknob, she shook it as hard as she could then pounded her other fist against the wall. She didn't even dent it. Even the walls were werewolf proof.

"Damn it, Kearnan. Let me out of here!"

Silence answered her.

Turning, fists clenched at her sides, Serena leaned back against the door, searching the room for another way out. Before her, dust motes danced in the light streaming through the skylight. She looked up. Glass was easy to break. And it was only about ten feet to the ceiling.

Quickly, she crouched then sprang upward, her fingers reaching for the thin decorative strips around the window frame. Letting all her weight hang from her right hand, she clenched her fist and punched the glass.

Pain exploded out from her knuckles as she fell back to the floor. "Shit, shit, shit!"

Not a single crack marred the glass.

"Damn you, Kearnan Gray! How long have you been planning this?" Serena howled as she flexed her hand and rubbed her knuckles. She glared at the door on the other side of the room. "Probably a closet—a small one."

Serena pushed herself away from the door and leaped across the room to the other door. Twisting the knob, she jerked it open. It slammed against the wall and ricocheted back shut. Muttering curses, she yanked it open again and stared into a small bathroom.

Combing her fingers through her hair, Serena grimaced when her fingers tangled in a snarl. Her braid had disintegrated sometime during the night. "I need a shower."

Serena glanced back over her shoulder. Who knew when he'd come back. She could at least get clean.

Sighing, she stepped first to the bathroom sink and filled the glass sitting there with water. She chugged it down, refilled it, and drained the glass a second time.

"Now I know why the wolves are always thirsty after they wake up. That drug causes major cotton mouth."

Turning to the shower, she turned on the spigots, adjusted the temperature, grabbed a washcloth from the shelf then stepped under the water. The hot cascade showering over her body washed away the aches and pains from the time she spent in the wolf den, but did nothing for the turmoil roiling through her mind. Kearnan Gray knew she was a werewolf. What was she going to do?

Grabbing the bottle of body wash from the shelf, she began to squeeze some onto the washcloth but paused when the floral scent filled the air. Turning the bottle over, she stared at the label. Her grandmother's homemade body wash. Dropping both it and the washcloth, she grabbed the shampoo. Her favorite brand. She looked at the final bottle on the shelf. So was the conditioner. Kearnan had taken them from her cabin; she was sure of it.

She screamed with frustration. "You cock-sucking son of a bitch! You shit-eating jackass. How long have you been planning this?"

Only the sound of rushing water answered her.

Serena slammed her fist into the wall. Three of the ceramic tiles cracked and fell to the floor. She kicked them across the shower stall. When they hit the opposite wall, two more tiles fell. "I hope the ass-fucking shithead has water leak down into the ceiling under this one, and he doesn't find out about it until the whole thing falls down on his head."

Bending over, she grabbed body wash from the floor of the shower and squeezed out a huge dollop onto a washcloth. Still muttering choice blasphemies concerning her boss's parentage, she began to scrub herself. A sharp stab in her groin reminded her of her other problem.

Serena dropped the washcloth and sank to her knees. "Gods, no, not now. Please, not now."

She slipped her fingers between her legs and moaned when she touched herself. Swollen. She was in heat.

Another stab of heat raced straight to her nipples, and they tightened into hard buds. Leaning her head back, she slid her fingers between her lips and touched her swollen clit. Shivering, as waves of pleasure raced through her body, she opened her eyes, her gaze focusing on the showerhead. Her fingers stopped moving when she realized it was removable.

Reaching up, she pulled the showerhead from its mount and directed the pulsating bursts of water from one nipple to the other. Both tightened, as spikes of heat radiated outward and downward through her stomach and into her groin. Cupping her left breast, she kneaded and squeezed. Her nipples tightened even more.

Moaning, Serena sank to the floor of the shower, slid onto her behind, and leaned back against the wall. Bending her knees, she braced her feet on the floor and opened her legs wide. When she reached down to brace her left hand on the floor, her hand bumped the bottle of body wash. Grabbing it, she turned it upside down and squeezed it all over her breasts, stomach, and pubic hair; the floral scent permeating the hot, humid air of the shower. Slowly, she began to rub the foam into her body. Then she directed the pulsating water directly against her swollen clit. Oh yes!

"Ahhhhhhh."

As her clit vibrated, her back arched, and she had to brace her free hand against the floor to keep her balance. What started as a whimper evolved into a full-bodied moan as she held the showerhead closer to her throbbing crotch. Her hips jerked forward, and she slid to her back. Switching the shower to her left hand, she slid the fingers of her right between her legs and began to rub.

"Oh, gods! Oh, gods! Oh, gods!"

The showerhead thunked to the floor as the orgasm ripped through Serena's body. Warm water ricocheted off the wall onto her shuddering body as waves of pleasure rolled outward from her groin. Palms braced flat against the floor, she clenched her internal muscles and experienced a second, milder orgasm.

Slowly, her shuddering decreased until she finally lay still. Panting, she pushed herself first into a sitting position then to her feet. She leaned against the wall to steady herself. Eventually, her breathing steadied. Using both hands, she replaced the showerhead, hanging onto the fixture until her legs could support her, and let the warm water sluice down her body. Her heat was just starting. This orgasm would satisfy her for a few hours or so, but then the lust would hit her again and again for the next week. Tonight would be the worst.

With a sigh, Serena let go of the showerhead. Bending, she groped for the shampoo bottle. She squeezed a dollop into her hand and smeared it into her hair. After about a minute of pushing the suds over her scalp, she stuck her head under the shower. She didn't bother with the cream rinse. Stepping out of the shower, she wrapped herself in a towel then reached for the brush on the back of the sink. She reached back and shoved the lid down on the toilet. Then she sank wearily onto the seat and began to work the tangles out of her wet hair.

A soft click from the other room caught her attention, and she rose to her feet. Carefully, she inched the bathroom door open.

Kearnan was setting a tray full of covered dishes on the dresser.

Her stomach growled when she caught the aroma of a steak grilled bloody rare, but she ignored it. Her freedom was more important than satisfying her hunger.

Snarling, she slammed the door open and stepped into the room. Before Kearnan could say anything, mist surrounded her and blurred her form.

"Don't do that, Serena."

She ignored him.

"Stubborn bitch." Kearnan lifted the dart gun in his left hand and fired.

Immediately the mist disappeared, and Serena collapsed on the floor, the dart imbedded in her thigh. Legs curled underneath her body, she pushed her torso up off the floor and locked her elbows. Her long, wet hair was plastered against her back and face. She bared her teeth and snarled, "You ass-licking buggerer. You cock-sucking whoreson."

Kearnan set the gun on the dresser and crossed the room. Kneeling at her side, he gathered her into his arms.

As much as she wanted to fight him, she couldn't. Her head lolled back on his shoulder, and she stared into his eyes. "Why? Why are you doing this to me?"

Gently, Kearnan laid her on the bed and brushed wet strands of hair out of her eyes. "Isn't it obvious? I've fallen in love with you."

Chapter Five

ꝏ

Serena woke up handcuffed to the bed. She twisted her neck and looked first at one confined wrist then rolled her head and looked at the other. She gave both of them an experimental tug.

"Would you like a drink of water?"

Serena froze at the sound of Kearnan's voice and swept the room with her gaze.

He was standing in a shadowed corner leaning against the wall.

"I'll take your silence for a yes," he said as he poured water into a glass and carried it to her. Bending over, he lifted her head and held the glass to her lips.

Her nostrils flared as the scent of his cologne enveloped her, but she gulped half the water down.

"Feel better now?"

Serena jerked her face away, and a snarl erupted from her throat. "As if you care. Why am I chained like this? Some perverse dream of yours, asshole? Is this the only way you can get a woman into your bed, handcuffing her to it?"

Kearnan set the glass down, crossed his arms over his chest, and grinned down at her. "When you decided to change and attack me, you left me no choice. Stretched out the way you are, you can't change into your wolf form. It's a physically impossibility for a wolf to be spread-eagled on its back the way you are. If you can't change into a wolf, I won't have to keep knocking you unconscious. Besides, you're so—tempting like this. Do you have any idea how stimulating, how arousing it is for me to see you like this, laid out before me like a gourmet meal. Your nipples are hard and pointed, begging for my mouth. Your stomach is smooth, perfect for licking and kissing. Your legs, gods, Serena, but your legs are beautiful. So perfectly toned. Are you ticklish behind the knees? How will you react if I kiss you there?"

"Shut up!" she growled.

Kearnan ignored her. "Are you wet yet, Serena? I'm going to taste you tonight. I'm going to lay myself between your legs and suck the sweetness of your cunt until you scream for me to bury my cock inside of you."

Serena barred her teeth and snarled. "Dream on, motherfucker. I have news for you, these handcuffs aren't going to hold me."

Lifting both wrists, Serena jerked them forward.

The metal handcuffs shrieked against the wrought iron railings of the bed's headboard, but they held. She jerked her wrists again—harder. The handcuffs—and the bed railings—held.

As Serena struggled against her bonds, Kearnan grinned down at her. "You can struggle all you want, sweetheart, but those handcuffs are stainless steel lined with titanium. European police use them to transport suspected terrorists."

"I—am—not—your—sweetheart, fuck head!" Serena growled through clenched teeth. She strained against the handcuffs until the tendons stood out on her neck. Her muscles began to burn, and she could feel the skin on her wrists begin to chafe.

A trace of anger crept into Kearnan's voice. "Serena, I padded the cuffs, but you could still hurt yourself if you keep struggling."

"I will not..." she began. Before she could finish, a sharp pang of heat stabbed her groin. Serena tried to clamp her legs together; but, because her ankles were also chained to bedposts, she was unable to do so. Another jolt of heat raced through her body. Her hips arched off the bed.

"Ahhhhhhhhh," she moaned. Tears leaked from the corners of her eyes.

Kearnan sat down beside her and brushed the hair away from her face.

"Now look what you've done. I told you to relax. All your struggling has brought on an attack sooner than it should have."

Serena snapped at him.

Kearnan yanked his hand away.

Another bolt of fire exploded between her legs, and Serena's hips jerked off the bed again. "Damn you, Kearnan Gray. Let me go."

He caressed her cheek then cupped her face in his hands. "Shhhh. I can't do that, Serena. Stop struggling and try to relax. I'll take care of you." Leaning over, he kissed her forehead once as threaded his fingers through her hair. Then, after kissing both her eyes, he trailed his lips down her cheek to her mouth and nibbled her lips.

When his lips parted hers, she bit him, clamping her teeth shut on his bottom lip, biting until she drew blood.

Kearnan froze, not even trying to free himself.

Another spasm of heat ripped through Serena's body, and she was forced to release his lip. After the spasm passed, she licked his blood off her lips, barred her teeth, and glared at him.

The rusty taste of his blood sent more heat surging through her veins.

Kearnan wiped the blood from his lip with the back of his hand and stared down at her. "Why do you keep fighting me?"

Her answer was half moan, half scream. "Why! You've kidnapped me, made me your prisoner. You have me chained like an animal."

Finally allowing some of his frustration to show, Kearnan slammed his fist down on the bedside table. "Damn it, what the hell else was I supposed to do, little bitch? Every time I've tried to talk to you about something other than the wolves, you'd change the subject then disappear. You made it apparent that you didn't like being alone with me. Even if other people were present, you'd stay as far away from me as possible. You even stay away from the staff picnics. Okay, if you weren't interested, I could deal. I'm not going to force myself on a woman who doesn't want me."

"I don't want you, asshole!" Serena screamed.

Leaning over, Kearnan fisted his hand in her hair and held her head still so she had no choice but to look into his eyes. "Wrong. You do want me, and we both know it. The last six months, every time I've talked to you you'd blush and catch your breath. You'd watch me when you thought I wasn't looking. When I did get you to stand still and listen to me, your nipples were soon trying to poke their way through your shirt to get to me. I see you squeeze your legs together and shift in your seat. More than once I saw your hand dip between your legs and rub your crotch. Always when you were near me. So don't tell me you aren't attracted to me."

Serena gritted her teeth. "I am not…"

Another stronger burst of prickly heat exploded in her groin. Her hips jerked again.

Releasing her hair, Kearnan leaned over her and rubbed her stomach, firmly kneading the muscles that clenched beneath his hand. Then he slid his hand down her quivering belly to his fingers lower—but not low enough.

"Do you want me, Serena?"

Closing her eyes, she groaned and lifted her hips into his palm.

Kearnan cupped her and applied pressure to where she wanted it most. His voice was more firm, more demanding. "Do you want me?"

Snarling, she opened her eyes. "Yes, damn you, you cocksucker. What other choice do I have. I want you. Are you satisfied now?"

His chuckle was arrogant. "I don't suck cocks. But I've dreamed of getting my mouth on your breasts for months. Bending over, he sucked her nipple into his mouth, twirled his tongue around it, then nipped it.

Moaning, she arched her breast further into his mouth. "Oh gods, yes."

His fingers slid between her slick folds. "You're so wet, love," he murmured against her breast. "So wet and wild." He lifted his fingers to his nose and inhaled.

Serena's breath caught in her throat. Kearnan's eyes seemed more golden than silver now. His face was tight with controlled passion.

"You smell like woman and sex and passion. I want you."

Then he licked his fingers.

Serena shuddered and moaned. Gods, what was he doing to her?

He slid his hand back between her thighs and pinched and rubbed her swollen clit. Her hips bucked against his hand. He bit down lightly on her nipple.

Serena screamed as an orgasm burst through her body.

After one last suckle of her nipple, Kearnan pulled his hand from between her legs and rose. Breathing deeply, he closed his eyes and struggled to regain total control of his body. He had to wait to take her, to bury his cock inside of her. She had to want him.

Still shuddering, Serena shifted, trying to get comfortable. She sniffed then looked over at Kearnan. "Okay, you've proved your point. You can give me a great orgasm. Let me go."

Opening his eyes, Kearnan smiled and shook his head. "No. I plan to prove to you that a man can give you the love you're looking for. That little bit of clitoral manipulation you just enjoyed you could have done for yourself. I'm not going to let you run away from me again. I'm more determined than any other lover you've had. I'm not like them. You can trust me."

Cheeks flaming, Serena turned her face towards the wall. How could he possibly know anything about her other lovers. "You don't know what you're talking about."

"I've done some checking. You ran away from your home never staying longer than six months anywhere until you got here. In each place, shortly after you took a lover, you left. You've stayed here on the preserve longer than you've stayed anywhere else since you left home. Just what did Alex Whitehorse do to drive you away?"

Serena snapped her head towards him. Her eyes widened when she saw he had taken his shirt off. The silvery hair on his muscular chest was almost invisible. A pale line slid down over his flat abdomen to disappear into the waistband of his jeans, jeans that had the button undone and the zipper part way down. More silvery hair peeked through.

Serena swallowed and tried to ignore the excited shiver that rolled up her spine.

Kearnan wasn't wearing any underwear.

Serena inhaled. The spicy tang of his arousal drifted to her nostrils.

She glanced at his face.

He was watching her, eyes hooded.

She could hear the pulse pounding in his neck. Her own breath caught in her throat. Her nipples ached. She stretched towards him.

The handcuffs rattled against the bed railings, and her anger returned. This jackass was ruining her life, a life he seemed to know too much about.

"How do you know about Alex?"

Kearnan smiled wickedly and pulled the zipper of his fly down further. "I hired a very good private investigator. Your mother was Native American—Cheyenne to be exact. Your father was white. Both of them were werewolves."

At her sharp intake of breath, Kearnan grinned and shook his head. "No, the private investigator didn't tell me that. You just confirmed it. Anyway, when you were six, your parents disappeared while skiing in the Rockies. It's believed they were killed in an avalanche, but their bodies were never found. Your Cheyenne grandparents raised you."

She turned her head away again and stared at the wall. More tears trickled down her cheeks. Why did he have to remind her about her parents? All those months of waiting for them to come back—and they never had.

"When you were eighteen," Kearnan continued, "you started dating Alex. Your entire pack knew to the hour when he first made love to you. You left home the two weeks later. Why?"

"It's none of your business," she mumbled to the wall.

"Serena," Kearnan continued in a firmer tone, one that demanded an answer, "why did you leave your pack?'

She turned her head back towards him. "How can you know anything about my pack?"

Did he tense?

"The dynamics can't be that different from a wolf pack. I'm an expert, remember?"

Serena turned her head away again. Damn cocksucker had an answer for everything.

"Did Alex hurt you?"

Serena snapped her head back towards Kearnan. "Hurt me? Alex would never hurt me or any other female. And yes, I made love with Alex—like humans, good old missionary position so it wasn't a true mating. I did not allow him to mount me, and I was not in heat. And you should have seen the look on his face when he realized he wasn't my first lover.

Why did I leave? I left because I don't want to marry Alex. He just can't accept that I don't love him. He's been courting me since I was sixteen. My grandfather had been Alpha before he died. Alex defeated all challengers for pack leadership, but he thought that marrying me would further cement his position."

"All you had to do was say no."

"Don't you think I tried? The only reason I went to bed with him was because I was hoping he'd lose interest in me when he found out I'd had sex with someone else first."

Serena turned her head back to the wall. Son-of-a-bitch not only had her chained to a bed, he was making her remember everything she wanted to forget.

Surprise inched its way into Kearnan's voice. "Surely your grandmother wouldn't force you to mate him if you didn't want to."

"Grandmother hasn't been the same since Grandfather died six years ago. She's worried about my future, and she's known Alex since he was a boy. Grandmother didn't understand why I couldn't fall in love with him. Alex is handsome, intelligent, and a good leader, everything a woman could hope for in a man."

His voice was closer. "But not you."

"I wanted to make Grandmother happy. I tried to love Alex for her sake, but I couldn't. And, when he wouldn't take no for an answer, I left. I had to. Grandmother was pressuring me to marry him, and Alex was planning the wedding."

"Why did you leave your other lovers?"

Serena closed her eyes. "They wouldn't have understood me. People don't believe in werewolves." Her voice hardened. "I thought I was safe here. I trusted you. I won't make that mistake again."

Kearnan's voice was suddenly gentle. "You can trust me, Serena. You just don't realize it—yet."

"Oh yeah," she snapped, "I can really trust you. You stripped me naked and chained me to a bed."

She ignored his rich chuckle.

"Look at me Serena," he commanded.

She refused to obey him.

"Look at me." There was no denying his demand.

She turned her head. "Okay, shithead, I'm looking."

He'd pulled the zipper down the rest of the way. His jeans hung loosely around his hips. A bulge was hidden just inside the open fly.

"The only thing holding them up is my cock, love."

Then Kearnan pushed the jeans down over his hips and stepped out of them. His uncircumcised cock jutted out in front of him, thick and heavy, its broad, smooth head completely free of the foreskin. As she watched, a drop of crystal clear liquid appeared. His cock jerked once, then once again.

Kearnan stepped to the side of the bed. His cock hung over her. "You want me, Serena. Even if I didn't have you chained to the bed, you'd spread your legs and beg me to shove my cock into you. Right now, you're wondering how it will feel. How much will it stretch you? Will it slide right in? Will you be able to handle all of it?"

Serena's heart beat faster. A funny feeling tumbled in the pit of her stomach. Everything he was saying was true. She wanted that thick, hard cock pounding into her as deeply as it would go. Inside, she began to melt. Silently, she cursed her body for betraying her.

Kearnan glanced up at the skylights then back to Serena. "The moon has risen. Can you feel its pull? You can't hunt, and that little bit of blood you got from my lip certainly didn't appease you. You're going to have to settle for sex, love. And I'm not going to let you go until your satisfied."

Grinding her teeth, Serena jerked against the handcuffs once more. Damn him. How she hated that he was right. She didn't need to look through the skylight to know the moon had risen. The heat racing through her veins and perspiration misting her body told her. And—those few drops of blood she'd swallowed when she'd bitten his lip only made her cravings worse.

She tensed her muscles and pulled against her restraints with all her strength. They didn't budge. Closing her eyes, she ground her teeth to stifle the moan that welled in her throat as a wave of heat raced through her bloodstream. She wanted his cock buried inside of her, and she didn't have a choice about it anyway. But, there was no reason he had to know that. Once he fucked her, he'd let her go. Then, she'd leave the preserve for good and never have to see Kearnan Gray ever again.

Serena turned her head to the side and glared at Kearnan. He was standing with his arms crossed over his chest, that damn impressive cock jutting out, a triumphant smile on his face. Gods, how she hated him. How could she have ever considered him attractive? "Okay, you win," she snarled. "I'll sleep with you. Now unchain me."

Kearnan grinned down at her. "No."

Sweat rolled into her eyes. Serena blinked then squirmed as the throbbing in her blood began to beat a syncopating rhythm in her groin. Damn him. He was going to keep her chained, spread-eagled on the bed. "Okay, then. Get it over with."

He chuckled as he sat down on the bed next to her. With a soft cloth he lifted from the bedside table, he wiped the perspiration from her forehead and out of her eyes.

"'Get it over with?' Were all your lovers that self-centered? Making love is not something to hurry. It's to be savored like a fine wine. No, now that I have you where I want you, I plan to take my time. And I promise, you will enjoy what I'm going to do as much or more than I will."

Kearnan dropped the cloth then cupped her breast with both hands and began to knead.

Her nipple was already pebbled, but Kearnan's firm handling tightened it further. Serena arched into his hand. "Ahhhhhhhhhh."

He turned his attention to her other breast. "You like that don't you? Someday, I'll show you the toys I have to enhance the pleasure you can experience through your nipples, but not this first time. Tonight the nipple clamps, dildoes, and other interesting toys stay in the drawer. No, tonight I'm going to introduce you to the pleasure you can experience with nothing more than a man's hands, mouth, and body. My hands, my mouth, and my body. We'll save the toys for another time."

"There isn't going to be another time," she gasped as Kearnan pinched her nipple between his finger and thumb, "and you can't keep me chained to this bed forever."

"I won't have to." His warm breath caressed her breast. "And we will make love again—and again and again. Now, just relax and let your body enjoy what I'm doing to it." Using both hands, he began to knead and squeeze her right breast until her nipple tightened even more. Then he lowered his head and sucked its peak into his mouth.

Heat stabbed straight to Serena's groin, and she arched her entire body off the bed. She sobbed as he turned his attention to her other breast. "Please, I need you to…"

"Patience, love," he interrupted between nips and tugs to her left nipple. "You need me to love you the way you deserved to be loved." Then he covered her mouth with his.

This time, Serena didn't bite. Instead she sucked his tongue into her mouth, caressing and stroking it with her own. She moved restlessly under his insistent strokes, trying to guide his hands to the ache between her thighs.

When she didn't succeed, she bucked in frustration.

Chuckling, Kearnan lifted his mouth from hers. He nipped her neck then kissed it. The nips and kisses trailed down her neck and shoulder to breast then back up her shoulder and neck to her mouth. Then he switched his nips and kisses to the other side of her face and torso.

Sensations Serena had never experienced surged through her as wet kisses followed sharp nips. Any thoughts of the hunt and thrill of the kill were gone, replaced by sexual lust stronger and more aching than she'd ever experienced. And, even though his hands and mouth never slid below her waist, she could feel her orgasm building. One more nip to an overly sensitive nipple would send her over the edge.

"Are you ready to come, yet, little wolf?" he teased as he nibbled up the column of her neck to suck on her ear. Then he lapped a wet trail around her neck and across her shoulder to her breast. He lapped it—top, bottom, sides—avoiding the nipple.

Frustrated, she moaned and arched her back, trying to guide her nipple to his mouth. "Pleeeeeeeease."

With a deep chuckle, he latched onto her nipple, wrapped his tongue around it, then sucked on it stopping only to bite gently. He dipped one finger between her thighs and stroked—once.

Serena shattered, the headboard of the bed rattling as she jerked on the handcuffs, only her head, shoulders, and heels touching the bed as she arched into his hand and mouth.

"That's it, sweetheart," he murmured, "come for me."

Serena closed her eyes and drowned in the waves of pleasure surging through her body.

Chapter Six

ജ

When Serena opened her eyes, Kearnan was sitting next to her, his hip brushing hers, his left hand braced on the bed between her spread thighs. He shifted slightly, and the soft hairs on his arm brushed against the inside of her thigh.

She glared at him. "Okay, the orgasm was great. Now let me go."

Kearnan threw back his head and laughed.

She gnashed her teeth. "Stop laughing at me, jerk!"

His grin flashed white when he looked back down at her. Gesturing towards the luminescent light dancing about the room, he said, "The moon is still high in the sky. Time for your next lesson."

Her stomach muscles quivered with anticipation. "What lesson?"

Kearnan didn't answer. Sliding off the bed, he knelt on the floor and simply buried his face between her legs. As he inhaled, a look of intense pleasure appeared on his face. "You smell hot, love, hot and molten." He slid his tongue between her folds for a long, slow lap. "And you taste of fire. Hot, passion-filled fire."

Serena's thighs tensed then quivered.

Steel handcuffs shrieked against iron railings.

"Oh gods!"

The muscles in Serena's stomach clenched as she arched her hips into Kearnan's face.

He lapped again then slurped. "Ambrosia, love. Pure ambrosia. You taste so good. I can't get enough of you." His hands slid under her ass cheeks and lifted her closer to his mouth.

Moaning, Serena pumped her hips, pushing her cunt up against Kearnan's smooth tongue. When he scrapped his teeth against her aching clit, she sobbed. When he nipped it, she screamed and pumped her hips harder.

Kearnan sucked harder, drawing her clit into his mouth, stabbing and twirling it with his supple tongue. When he nipped it again, Serena shattered with another orgasm. Then, when she'd barely stopped shuddering, he rolled onto the bed, stretched out on his stomach between her legs, and started all over again.

Gasping for breath between her moans, Serena gritted her teeth and looked down her body to watch Kearnan's head bob and shift between her thighs, his silvery hair a startling contrast to her black pubic curls. Prickly whiskers rasped against the delicate skin of her inner thighs. His tongue stabbed and lapped. She longed to close her thighs tight against his head and hold his face with its magical tongue between them forever.

Kearnan raised his head and stared into her eyes. "You taste better than the finest wine. He closed his eyes and inhaled deeply. "By the seven hells, I have never smelled or tasted anything like you. I just can't get enough." Lowering his head, he lapped more moisture from her slick folds.

Serena rolled her head back and arched her shoulders off the bed. When had she ever been so wet? When had she ever come so much? Why was this man able to affect her so?

Again, Kearnan sucked her aching nub between his teeth and nipped.

The entire bed shook when Serena came again.

Her heart racing, her breath coming in short gasps, curls of hair falling into her eyes, Serena raised her head and looked at Kearnan.

He grinned at her then dropped his gaze back to her cunt. "You're beautiful down here, Serena, soft and silky as the most delicate red rose, yet sweet and hot, passion-filled and eager for my lips and tongue. Come for me again, love. Feed me with your own sweet honey."

Kearnan lowered his mouth and began a new assault.

Serena moaned and lifted her hips to his mouth.

Propping himself on his forearms, Kearnan watched Serena's writhing figure as another orgasm wracked her body. In the last hour, moans, keens, and howls had erupted from her mouth, but no words of affection—or forgiveness. Damn, but she was stubborn. She had to care for him, at least a little. In the last six months, he'd caught her staring at him more than once. He couldn't have read those furtive glances incorrectly. Serena was attracted to him. He was sure of it. *What will she do when I let her go? Will she stay? Or will she run from me too? Do I mean as little to her as those other men in her life? Does she see me as a threat to her freedom? What will I do if I can't convince her to stay?*

Kearnan closed his eyes. He'd sworn never to become permanently involved with any woman, yet Serena had burrowed her way into his heart. Now, no matter how hard he tried, he hadn't been able to dislodge her. When his friendly overtures and careful attempts at courtship hadn't had any effect, locking her in this room and handcuffing her to the bed had been his last resort. But, he couldn't keep her chained to the bed forever. He had only one option, to redouble his efforts and sexually satiate her to the point where she'd be physically unable to leave.

As Serena's orgasm subsided and her trembling body relaxed, Kearnan slid two fingers inside of her and began sucking on her clit.

Again, the muscles in her thighs contracted.

Kearnan sat up and released both her ankles. Turning back to her, he once again stretched out between her legs, slid his hands beneath her behind, and lifted her to his mouth. She clamped her thighs around his head, thrust her crotch into his face, and rode his mouth and tongue until she came again.

As Serena legs dropped from his shoulders and shuddered with yet another orgasm, Kearnan slid up her body and kissed her. The hours he'd spent playing with Serena, teasing her into orgasm after orgasm had stretched his self-control to the limit. Right now, his balls were fiery with need, and his cock felt ready to explode. He needed to be inside of her, but he couldn't just take her like this, without her consent even though she was completely at his mercy.

Kearnan trailed his tongue over her shoulder and up her neck then stared down into her face. He had to ask her for permission to continue, even if his balls did explode. "Serena, should I stop? Do you want me to let you go?"

Awash in a sea of emotion and physical sensations as another orgasm rippled through her body, Serena barely realized that Kearnan's caresses had stopped and he was talking to her. Slowly, her senses returned, and she blinked to focus. Kearnan lay atop her over-sensitized, tingling body, staring intently into her eyes. His mouth moved again. What was he saying?

Her brain began to function, and his words registered. *Stop? Now? Is he nuts? I've just experienced the most mind-blowing sex of my life, and he hasn't even slid his cock into me yet. He can't stop, not now.*

"If you stop now, I'll rip your heart out," Serena growled. Lifting her head, she captured Kearnan's mouth with hers and sucked his tongue into her mouth. At the same time, she bucked against him once. The head of his cock slid along her sopping folds. Her legs free, she lifted them and wrapped them around his waist.

Kearnan groaned and entered her with one, hard thrust.

Moaning into his mouth, Serena wrapped her tongue around Kearnan's and clamped her internal muscles around his cock. He was so long, so thick, so hard! She felt stretched, completely filled. Again she clenched her muscles. She felt his cock jerk.

Kearnan's mouth left hers to trail a line of nips down the side of her neck to her shoulder.

As Kearnan started to suck on her breast, Serena gasped, "You're so hard, like a rock pushed up inside me. You feel so goooood." She rocked her hips, and he settled deeper. She moaned. "Fuck me. Now. Hard and deep."

Lifting his head, Kearnan stared into her face. "My bitch, my beautiful, passionate bitch. I love you."

Then he began to pump his hips. When his cock slid out, her muscles relaxed. Then he thrust back into her, and her muscles had to stretch to accommodate the thickness of his cock as he filled her—again and again and again.

Serena pumped her hips and tried to match his rhythm. but he didn't cooperate with straight forward, evenly placed thrusts. Instead, he pushed his hips against hers, circled them, and swayed them unrhythmically. It was the greatest sex she'd ever experienced. The handcuffs chaining her to the bed shrieked as they slid against the iron bed railings.

"Damn, Serena, I love you," Kearnan breathed into her mouth. Resting his full weight on her, he reached up with both hands and snapped the releases on the handcuffs.

"Ahhhhhhhhhh." Tingling needles shot up and down her arms, but she ignored them and buried her hands in his thick hair. Then she slid them down his back to caress his muscular ass. She dug into each cheek with her sharp nails.

"Harder. Deeper," she moaned. She bit his neck.

With the pleasure/pain from Serena's bite rippling through his muscles straight to his groin, Kearnan gasped and plunged harder, pushing Serena up the mattress as he slammed his cock as deeply as he could. She was wet, slick, and tighter than he'd dreamed possible for a woman with some sexual experience. Her strong internal muscles grabbed at his cock, squeezed it, sought to milk it until he was drained dry.

"Hell, you're wet." He nipped her neck. "You're tight and slippery. That's it, squeeze my cock harder. Milk it, Serena. Make me come. I want to explode inside of you, fill you with my come.

He rammed her harder.

She tightened her legs around his waist and tried to pull him deeper inside.

Kearnan kissed her again. "Now, love, I can't last any longer. I'm going to explode."

"Yes," she moaned. "Come. Come in me. Fill me up."

Kearnan raked his teeth along the side of her neck. "Mine, you're mine, Serena."

He drove his cock into her as deeply as he could, tensed, and shuddered. With a groan, he collapsed on top of her.

Serena's entire body sang. Her clit already over-sensitized by Kearnan's almost constant licking and sucking felt as if thousands of tiny, sharp needles were rubbing against it. The friction caused by each stroke of his cock inflamed her delicate, internal muscles until they wept constant moisture. The silky hairs on his chest brushed her aching nipples, stimulating and exciting them.

Serena rolled her head from side to side. Her body felt ready to explode. "I'm going to come. Oh Gods, it feels so good!"

Finally, Kearnan plunged into her so hard that her head thunked against the top of the bed. When molten heat drenched the muscles gripping his cock so tightly that they melted and waves of intense, rippling pleasure rolled outward from her groin, Serena wrapped her arms around Kearnan to anchor herself against the storm of ecstasy raging through her body.

What seemed like a year later, Serena let her legs fall from around Kearnan's waist and nuzzled his shoulder. She had never been so sexually replete and satisfied in her entire life.

With a sigh, Kearnan rolled onto his back, pulling her along.

Serena settled her head above his heart. Exhausted, she snuggled against him, nuzzling the silky, silver hairs on his chest. Completely relaxed and satiated from his attentions, Serena drifted towards sleep.

Wrapping his arm tighter, Kearnan pulled her closer. "I'm sorry."

Serena pressed closer, throwing one leg over his thighs, her arm over his waist. "For what?" she mumbled against his chest.

He brushed the top of her head with his lips. "For chaining you to the bed."

Serena yawned then chuckled. She nipped his nipple. "I'm not."

Serena woke and stretched. She groaned. She ached in places that hadn't ever ached before. Kearnan certainly hadn't missed an inch of her body as he'd made love to her.

Kearnan.

Closing her eyes, Serena smiled. What a night! Kearnan should have chained her to the bed months ago.

Thank the gods she was a werewolf and not just a human woman. Kearnan's autocratic handling would have had the majority of human women stomping out of the house on principle once he'd released them. Not her. No way. Kearnan had acted just like a male werewolf—domineering and possessive.

Serena snuggled her face into her pillow and inhaled. Kearnan's scent tickled her nose. *Gods, what a man,* she thought. *Now I know why those other men didn't satisfy me. They didn't know how. I needed a man who did. I needed Kearnan.*

With another groan, Serena shifted, and her behind brushed against something soft and furry. Rolling over, she found herself face to face with a large, silvery-gray wolf. Tongue lolling out, he stared at her. His tail thunked against the bed, twice.

Serena gaped and stiffened. Realization dawned. "Kearnan?"

Silvery mist swirled, and Kearnan was lying next to her.

Forgetting all about the aches in the delicate areas of her body, Serena shot to a sitting position and stared down at him.

Kearnan laced his fingers behind his head.

She punched him in the ribs. "You're a werewolf. You ass! Why didn't you tell me?"

Kearnan grunted from the force of her punch but the sigh that followed was contented. "I was afraid you'd run away from me too."

"Run away?"

He grinned. "You ran away from Alex and every other man you've dated. I didn't want to take a chance on losing you. Chasing you down would have been too much of a hassle."

Serena gaped at him. "Too much of a hassle! If you want something bad enough, you'll work to get it."

"And I worked very hard to get you. Do you know how long I've planned this? It took six months to get everything in place."

He continued to grin and stretched, his arms brushing against the iron railing of the headboard.

Serena's eyes narrowed. Conceited son of a bitch.

Far more swiftly than a normal human, she straddled him, reached up, and snapped the handcuffs around his wrists.

Kearnan stiffened then tested his strength against the handcuffs. They rattled against the iron railings. He glanced at Serena.

She sat on him, smiling triumphantly. "How does it feel to be totally helpless and at someone else's mercy?"

Kearnan's eyelids drooped, and his cock stirred against her butt. "Why don't you show me?"

With a low chuckle, Serena leaned over and pinched his nipple. His flaring nostrils and sharp intake of breath spurred her on. Her mouth followed her fingers, and she wrapped her tongue around first one nipple then the other until he was squirming under her. His erection brushed against the crack of her behind. Her nipples tightened and her crotch grew wet.

"How do you like me sucking on your nipples? Does it feel as good for you as it did for me?" she mumbled against his chest between delicate nips and wet, sucking kisses.

"You can feel how I like it," he choked out. He rolled his hips, slapping his cock against her ass.

Lifting her head, Serena shifted off of him, cocked her head to the side, and smiled at the erection rising from its nest of silver hair. "I like it hard and deep. How hard can your cock get?"

Before Kearnan could answer, she leaned over and sucked the head into her mouth.

The iron railings of the headboard screamed as the handcuffs rattled. The entire bed shuddered as his hips jerked off the bed.

Reaching down, Serena cupped his balls in her hand, rolled them around, and squeezed them.

He tried to thrust his cock deeper into her mouth.

"Oh, no," she mumbled around a mouthful of cock in a low voice. "You tortured me. Now it's my turn to play."

After twirling her tongue around the head, she lapped a wet trail down one side of his cock then back up the other.

Again, she sucked the head into her mouth. Again, she trailed her tongue down one side and up the other. "Ummmm. Better than an ice cream cone. More like a lolly pop, my own personal sucker. What flavor are you?"

She sucked on the head again. "Passion fruit."

Kearnan clenched his fists and jerked against the handcuffs again. The railings rasped and groaned. "Damn it, Serena. Stop playing."

She chuckled. "But I like to play. You got to play with me." She sucked his cock deep into her mouth, but before he could thrust deeper, she pulled back and tickled the base of the head with her tongue. Then she nibbled her way to its base and sucked first one ball and then the other into her mouth.

Hips jerking, Kearnan groaned.

Serena blew on his balls. "Do you like this?" she teased. "Does it make you harder? Are you ready to come?" A deeper growl was his answer.

Serena licked his balls—first one then the other. She sucked them into her mouth and rolled her tongue around them. Lifting her head, she looked into his eyes. "This is for handcuffing me to the bed." Then she bent over and nipped him at the base of his cock—hard.

The iron railings on the headboard shrieked then gave way. Kearnan grabbed Serena, tossed her onto her back, captured both hands in one of his, and rolled on top of her. He spread her thighs with his knees, and ground his cock against her wetness. The handcuff dangling from his wrist rubbed against her forearms.

He stared down at her. "You bit me. You bit my dick!"

"You kidnapped me and handcuffed me to the bed without asking," Serena snapped back as she bucked and tried to dislodge him. "I'll bite you again if I have to."

A slow smile appeared on Kearnan's face. "Promise?" He dipped his head and nipped her neck. Then he slid his knees between her legs, parted her legs wider, and plunged inside.

Serena arched into his thrust, answering it with her own. She shuddered as he nipped her shoulder. Kearnan was wilder than he had been last night, and she loved it. His hips ground into hers, and he growled when she seemed to try to shift away from him.

He stopped moving and rested all of his weight on her. "Mine. You're mine, Serena. Say it."

"Yours, Kearnan. Only yours."

An arrogant smile on his lips, Kearnan began to move again.

Serena let herself go. Her orgasm was shattering.

When she dug her nails into Kearnan's back, he pumped hard twice and stiffened. Then, burying his face in her neck, he relaxed.

Chapter Seven

ꟷ

As Kearnan rolled off of her and onto his back, Serena snuggled against his side, nuzzled his chest, and inhaled. The odor of man and sex teased her senses. How she loved the way he smelled! The soft hair under his arm tickled her shoulder. She licked the fine sheen of perspiration from his skin. "Ummm." He tasted pretty good, too.

Her stomach growled.

Kearnan's chuckle rumbled. "Hungry?"

Serena nipped his chest. "I spent almost an entire day and night in a wolf den. I'm barely out for half an hour, tired and hungry, barely able to think straight, you kidnap me. Except for a drugged mug of tea and a couple of glasses of water, I haven't had anything else to drink or eat in over thirty-six hours." She pushed up onto an elbow and looked down at him. "Instead of feeding me, you handcuffed me to the bed and had your evil way with me. You're lucky I haven't started gnawing on your leg."

Kearnan grinned. "Don't blame me for not having anything to eat. I had a tray of food with me the first time I came in here. You're the one who decided to attack me instead of eating."

Serena's stomach growled even more loudly. "Well, I'm not attacking you now. Feed me."

As Kearnan sat up, Serena scooted over to the edge of the bed. The handcuff dangling from his right wrist bumped her thigh. She glanced back to the bent iron railings of the headboard. "You broke the bed."

An arrogant smile appeared on Kearnan's face as he unfastened first one then the other handcuff and tossed them on the bed. Wrapping his arm around Serena's waist, he pulled her onto his lap and kissed her. "It was worth it."

His hand slid between her thighs.

She was still swollen and wet.

He nuzzled her neck. "You're still in heat."

Serena's stomach rumbled again. She nipped his shoulder and slid off his lap. "I'll be in heat for the rest of the week. Sex later. Food now."

Turning, she sashayed into the bathroom and closed the door behind her. She had more than one need to satisfy.

Kearnan's nostrils flared as he watched her swaying hips. After the door closed, he lifted his fingers to his nose and inhaled. The rich, musky aroma shot bolts of electricity straight to his groin, and his cock stirred. Chuckling, he dropped his hand and rose to his feet. Serena was right. Food now. They both needed to keep up their strength.

As Kearnan rose, his sensitive ears registered the sound of rushing water. Serena must be taking a shower. That would give him time to stop in his room to grab some clean clothing for both of them. As much as he loved seeing Serena naked, he'd never be able to control himself long enough for her to eat. The scent of her heat was far too enticing.

"I'll be in the kitchen," he called and headed out the door. "I have a couple of steaks in the refrigerator."

Serena's stomach growled at the sound of Kearnan's voice. She hoped they were big steaks.

Grabbing the shampoo, she squeezed a dollop onto her hand. As she worked it through her hair, her mind drifted back to her thoughts from earlier that morning and Kearnan's arrogant high-handedness. How she loved it! Her werewolf side reveled in his domination. Male werewolves could become very arrogant and heavy-handed when claiming a mate, especially if she was in heat. Kearnan had been far more gentle than most male werewolves would have been. She'd seen some female werewolves emerge from a heat mating battered and bruised. Their males hadn't been unscathed either. In every case, both had been extremely happy.

"Ah, hell, Serena. Be honest with yourself," she muttered to herself. "You've been fantasizing about Kearnan for months. True you never pictured yourself handcuffed to a bed." She shivered. Handcuffed to the bed. Gods, but the sex was better than anything she'd ever imagined. She rinsed the shampoo out of her hair and grabbed the conditioner. "And I thought he was human. Why didn't I know he was a werewolf?"

Because you spent as little time as possible with him, ditz, answered a snippy voice in her head, *and when you were around him, so were the wolves. Their presence hid his.*

"But what about the staff meetings," Serena muttered back. "The wolves weren't at those."

Her stomach rumbled even more loudly.

She sighed. "I can figure this out later. Time to eat."

After rinsing her hair again, Serena turned off the water and stepped out of the shower. She wrapped herself in a towel, bent over, and wrapped her hair in another.

Straightening, she spied her reflection in the bathroom mirror. A now frowning Serena stared back at her. She should have realized Kearnan wasn't human. Damn, but she'd worked with him for three years. Wolves or no wolves, he shouldn't have been able to hide his true scent from her that long.

Serena pulled the towel from her hair and began to comb it. She'd thought a human had played her body with such skill and finesse. Kearnan certainly acted like a human, even in bed. He'd had her helpless and spent hours playing with her body to prove his point about human love. Still, he'd released her and offered to let her leave before making love to her. The sex hadn't been the mindless, hormone driven mating it could have been.

But Kearnan wasn't completely human. He was a werewolf, like her. This morning, when she'd bitten his cock, his reaction had been immediate. She still couldn't believe he'd had the strength to break the iron bars of the bed's headboard.

A shiver danced up and down her spine then dove for her groin. Even satiated as she was at the moment, she shuddered, anticipating the next time they made love.

Dropping the comb, Serena went back into the bedroom. Next time. Her heat would lessen rapidly now that the moon was waning, but she'd still need sex to satisfy the urges flowing through her blood. Her only other option was the thrill of the hunt and taste of warm blood at the kill. But, sex with Kearnan was better. Not even the thrill of the hunt, the smell of fear rolling off of her prey, or the taste of warm blood pumping into her mouth when she made her kill was better. Kearnan had concentrated on her pleasure first, made her come over and over before he satisfied himself. He told her he loved her. He was a man to keep, a werewolf to keep. He'd claimed her as his, declared she was his. Only one question remained in her mind. Why hadn't he mounted her the way a werewolf claims his mate?

"Why bother yourself worrying, Serena," she muttered to herself as she loosened the towel and let it drop to the floor. "He's a male. As Grandmother always said, "Considering how predictable our males are, they're damn unpredictable."

Looking around the room, she spotted the clothing she'd worn two days ago lying on the bed- freshly laundered and folded.

She grinned. "He does laundry. If he's a good cook, he can be as unpredictable as he wants. I'll keep him anyway."

After placing Serena's clothing on the bed, Kearnan had taken the time to stop in his room for a pair of clean sweat pants and tee shirt so he was just dropping a couple of thick steaks onto the broiler when Serena joined him in the kitchen.

She wrapped her arms around his waist from behind and hugged him. "Smells good."

He leaned back into her and poked a steak. "I just put them on."

"And you can flip mine over right away. I like my steak rare—the bloodier the better."

Kearnan flipped the steak and said, "Fresh lettuce and other stuff for salad is in the fridge."

Serena snorted. "Rabbit food! No thanks. Just meat for me—lots of it."

"A woman after my own heart."

Serena hugged him again, and a spicy scent enveloped her. She inhaled. Then she stretched up on her toes and sniffed the back of his neck. "It's the cologne. Damn it, your cologne hides the werewolf scent. That's why I didn't know."

"You better step back if you want your steak bloody rare, Sweetheart. My mind wanders in other directions when you're sniffing me."

Serena stepped back. "Why use cologne to hide your scent? Without it, the only ones who would know would be other werewolves."

Kearnan dropped the steaks onto two plates, grabbed them, and headed for the table. "Because I don't want other werewolves to know what I am. I like my privacy."

Serena followed him across the kitchen. "Who would bother you? A male werewolf who wants to be left alone is left alone."

Kearnan set the plates on the table, turned, jerked Serena into his arms, and kissed her—thoroughly. He sucked her tongue into his mouth and mated it to his while he cupped her buttocks and pulled her against his erection. When he finally released her, Serena's knees wobbled, and she was forced to grab his forearms for support.

Kearnan buried his face in her hair and inhaled deeply. "Less talk," he growled, "more eat. Your scent is driving me wild."

With those words, he guided Serena to a chair and set her down. The tantalizing aroma of seared steak wafted upward. When her stomach roared again, all thoughts not dealing with food fled her mind.

When Serena stabbed her knife and fork into her steak, Kearnan relaxed his guard, sat down, and started on his own meal. The last thing he needed right now was Serena asking too many pointed questions. She hadn't rebelled when he claimed her, and she showed no inclination to run away from him. She could find out the truth about his past and ancestry after their relationship was on solid footing—preferably after three or four children had been born—maybe.

Chapter Eight

ꟷ

Alex Whitehorse reached over and changed the radio station—again.

"Damn it, Alex, let the radio alone. It's not like we have a wide selection with all these mountains around us."

"If I want your opinion, Josh, I'll ask for it. You should have stayed at home to care for the pack. I could have driven down myself. How much farther?"

Josh switched the radio station back to its original station. Dwight Yokum's voice filled the SUV. "According to the directions we got at that minimart, we take the next left onto Oak Canyon Road then another left when we get to the Oak Canyon Preserve sign. And the pack is fine. The council won't allow someone to assume your position just cause we're gone for a couple of days. You need to learn to relax."

"I'll relax when you pay attention to your driving and don't miss the turn."

"You can not force Serena to mate you, Alex. Why don't you choose someone else? There's not an unmated woman in the pack who would turn you down."

Alex turned to face the woman sitting behind Josh. "Because twelve years ago, when I defeated the other two contenders for pack leadership, you and the other members of the council convinced me to wait for Serena to grow up and then choose her for my mate. As granddaughter of the last pack leader, mating her would cement my position. I agreed. I liked Serena. She was an intelligent girl who seemed interested in pack responsibilities. She knew I was only waiting for her to be old enough to mate."

Alex continued to stare into the woman's eyes. "Before Serena left, she claimed I didn't love her. Why would she say that? I do so love her. There is no other female I'd want for my mate, to be Alpha female. When she sees me, she'll know she was wrong. Why else would I chase her half way across the country?"

"Ah, hell, Alex," Dave Forrest cajoled from the back seat, "it's only been three hundred miles."

"Shut up, Dave," Alex snapped. "The last thing I want is advice from an Omega."

Dave immediately shrank back into his seat and looked out the window.

"A good leader does not belittle his followers," George TwoBears admonished.

Smashing his fist into his palm, Alex jerked himself around and stared straight ahead. He eyed the dashboard—wishing he could punch it to relieve some of his frustration. But, if he did, his fist would shatter the metal and plastic, undoubtedly causing some kind of malfunction. This SUV was the one luxury he'd allowed himself since becoming Alpha. He didn't want to break it. Worse, George was right. He should never have lashed out at Dave. Like Josh, he'd been a friend since they were all boys.

Alex clenched his fists tighter. Damn but he had more important things to do than chase after Serena. Why was she being so fickle? What did she mean he didn't love her. Of course he did.

"No matter where his place in pack hierarchy is, each member of the pack is important," George continued.

"Damn it," Alex snarled, "you're not even pack. If not for Alesandra…"

"You agreed with the council that he could stay," Alesandra interjected.

"She's right," Josh added.

"I don't need advice from my Beta, either."

Josh stomped on the brake. Tires squealed as the SUV slid to a stop in the middle of the road. After jamming the gearshift into park, he jerked around in his seat until he faced Alex. "Wrong. Giving you advice is my job, and you used to listen to me. Ever since Serena ran away, you've become more and more obsessed with her. I agreed to help you find Serena, to find out once and for all if she will mate you. If she doesn't, you have to choose someone else. The pack is getting restless. If you weren't such a powerful fighter, at least three different members would have challenged you by now."

Alex's fingers sank through the armrest. "Who are they?"

"Enough," Alesandra commanded. "No one is going to challenge you, Alex. Josh, lets go. We have a journey to finish."

The two men glared at each other for a moment. Dropping his eyes first, Josh turned his attention back to the road. Easing the SUV back into gear, he took his foot off the brake and continued down the lonely road.

Behind Alex, George TwoBears turned his gaze to Alesandra. *If I were a woman, I would not mate him either.*

Alesandra chuckled then ignored the angry glare Alex tossed over his shoulder. Telepathic communication was especially handy when one didn't want one's conversation overheard. *If you were a woman, my love, Alex would take one look at your hairy body and run howling the other way.*

George grinned. *You don't seem to mind. Besides, our women are no more hairy than yours.*

Alesandra answered his grin with one of her own. Ever since George had staggered out of the forest and collapsed bleeding from multiple wounds on her cabin porch, her life had taken on new meaning. She had a new reason to live. And, with that reason came the realization that she had made a mistake with Serena and Alex.

She leaned her head back and closed her eyes. *It's all my fault, George. I thought Serena was falling in love with Alex, that he would be the perfect mate for her. If her parents had lived, they'd have been the Alpha male and female after her grandfather and me. I wanted the same for Serena. In my mind, she was the best choice for Alpha female. If one of the other males had defeated Alex, I'd have wanted her to mate him. But Alex defeated them easily, and he led the pack quite well, exactly as my husband had groomed him to do after Serena's parents died. Then Serena came of age.*

Alesandra opened her eyes and stared out the window at the passing scenery—a seemingly endless forest of trees, oak, pine, hemlock, birch.

George sat quietly, his silence encouraging her.

When she was young, I encouraged Serena to spend time with Alex, even when she didn't want to. I was wrong.

George shifted in his seat, seeking a more comfortable position for his large form. *She is much younger than he is.*

Alesandra nodded. *Yes. That was one of my mistakes. Werewolf teenagers are not all the different from regular humans. For all her intelligence, Serena was too immature to appreciate what Alex wanted from her. At that time, all she saw was the envy of her friends because the pack Alpha was courting her. Maybe if she hadn't gone to his bed…*

George shook his head. *Alex does not impress me as the type of man to let anyone or anything keep him from what he wants. He wants Serena.*

She sighed. *I know, and I fear his reaction if she refuses to return with us.*

Alesandra shifted her gaze to Alex. He was handsome—his dark hair, dark eyes, and high cheekbones all bespoke his Cheyenne ancestry. Even the bump on the bridge of his nose where he'd broken it was appealing. And he was proving to be an excellent Alpha—even better than her own Michael had been. Alex took his responsibilities to the pack seriously, spending most of his time dealing with pack business. What little free time he had, he'd spent with Serena and her.

Alesandra's eyes widened. Alex had spent most of his free time courting Serena. That was it. Why hadn't she realized? Of course Alex was obsessed with Serena becoming his mate. If she refused, he had to go through the entire courting ritual all over again. More than a few unmated women had found their ways to his bed before Serena came of age but none since. Those women who would have been capable of assuming Alpha female responsibilities knew Alex wasn't interested in more than sex. They'd all chosen other mates since then. The only females available for mating were all younger. Alex didn't really know much about any of them.

If Serena wouldn't mate Alex, he'd have to take the time to find another woman who was not only compatible, one he could love, but who would also be strong enough to be Alpha female. With all his responsibilities to the pack, when would he find the time?

He's afraid, Alesandra thought to herself. *He's devoted the last twelve years of his life to the pack. If Serena says no, he'll have to court another woman, and he doesn't know how to begin. The available women in our pack are all young, and he doesn't have time to seek out available mates from other packs. He's not afraid for himself. He's afraid the pack will suffer if he gives it one iota less of his time.*

Chapter Nine

ꟗ

Kearnan cupped his mug in his hands and leaned back in his chair. He stretched his legs out under the table, spreading them to accommodate his growing erection, and sipped his coffee. More blood rushed to his cock as Serena's pink tongue slid up one side of each finger and down the other as she delicately licked beef juice from them. Kearnan swallowed—without coffee—when Serena sucked a finger into her mouth. Not so long ago, she'd been wrapping that tongue around his cock and sucking it into her wet mouth.

Shifting, Kearnan clenched his mug more tightly. No other woman had ever made him come so close to losing the control he fought to maintain. Earlier that morning, when Serena had bitten the base of his cock, the wolf in his soul had howled for release. The urge to dominate Serena, to demand her submission had almost overpowered him. Almost. He'd won the fight with his primitive side—barely. But he had controlled his wild side, and now he knew he would continue to do so. He had not allowed the wolf in his soul total control. Serena would be safe with him.

"Mmmmmmm. That was good." Serena stretched her arms over her head, arching her chest towards him.

Kearnan's attention slid to her breasts.

Her nipples poked eyes in the thin tee shirt she wore.

His now fully erect cock jerked.

"How can you drink that stuff?"

Kearnan's gaze returned to her face.

Fingers now laced behind her head, Serena smiled then wrinkled her nose.

His attention darted back to her chest as he sipped more coffee. "An acquired taste, but I like it."

Pulling her hands from behind her head, Serena rubbed her collarbone. Then, ever so slowly, she trailed her index finger down over the swell of her breast and flicked her extended nipple. Underneath the soft cotton of her shirt, her nipples became more pronounced.

Kearnan's gaze was glued to her chest.

She shifted in her chair.

Kearnan flared his nostrils and inhaled. "You spread your legs. I can smell your sex."

Her eyelids drooped, and Serena smiled a lazy smile. "I'm not wearing any underwear."

Coffee splattered on the table and floor as Kearnan dropped his mug. Confident in his ability to control himself, he erupted out of his chair and across the table.

Shoving dirty dishes out of his way, he leaned over and pulled Serena into his arms. Plates shattered and cutlery clanged to the floor as he dragged her back across the table into his arms.

She chuckled deep in her throat and wrapped her arms around his neck.

The musty aroma of her heat surrounded Kearnan.

Pulling her into his arms, his lips latched onto a cotton-covered nipple.

Serena arched into his mouth. "The dishes," she gasped. "There are bones on the floor."

"The hell with them," he mumbled against her breast.

Serena grabbed two handfuls of hair and jerked his head up. "Make love to me. Here. Now."

Kearnan jerked his head free. "No. Not this time. I want you in my room, my bed, my den."

"Yes." She lapped his neck.

Rising with Serena in his arms, Kearnan kicked his chair out of the way. It flew across the kitchen and bounced off the opposite wall, two legs shattering. He reached the door with one leap and shoved it open with his hip.

He was half way to the stairway when front door slammed open.

Serena staggered, grabbing onto the back of a wing chair for balance when Kearnan dropped her to her feet and turned to face the intruders. Raking her hair out of her face, she steadied herself then stepped to his side.

Four men faced them.

They parted to allow the old woman access to the house.

Serena stared. "Grandmother?"

Alex Whitehorse didn't give the older woman a chance to answer. "Get your stuff, Serena. You're coming home."

Serena fisted her hands on her hips. "Like hell. I'm staying here. If I wanted to come home, I'd have done so months ago."

Jaw set, Alex stepped forward. "Damn it. You've had long enough to find yourself or get to know yourself or whatever the hell else you had to do. It's time for you to accept your responsibilities to the pack."

"Serena," Kearnan interjected in a calm voice, "introduce me to your—friends."

Serena glared at their uninvited guests. No way was she going to let her old pack dictate her life. "Dr. Kearnan Gray, my grandmother, Alesandra Morning. To her left is Alex Whitehorse." Kearnan's muscles tensed under her hand. "The man to his left Josh Black. The man on the far right of my grandmother is Dave Forrest. I don't know the other man."

The last man crossed his arms over his chest and nodded. "George TwoBears. I am a friend of your grandmother's."

A quick slash of Alex's hand halted whatever else George wanted to say. "Enough. Come with us now, Serena."

She yanked her hand from Kearnan's arm and straightened to her full height. "I said no. I am not leaving. I have my work with the wolves, and—Kearnan loves me."

Her grandmother started.

Fists clenched at his sides, Alex stepped forward. "You'd choose him over me?"

Kearnan slipped an arm around Serena's waist and pulled her back against his chest. "You heard her. She stays with me. Leave. Now."

Alex stepped forward only to stop suddenly. He lifted his head, and his nostrils flared. Shock replaced his anger. "You're in heat."

Serena lifted her chin and glared at him.

Alex's voice grew louder. "I can smell you on him. You're in heat, and you let a man mount you!"

"I choose Kearnan," Serena snarled back.

"Stop. Now," Alesandra commanded, rapping her cane against the floor. When she had their attention, she walked forward slowly, pushing Alex to the side and halting a few feet before Serena. "This man is not for you, Serena. You know the—difficulties—that would be involved."

Serena hugged the arm Kearnan now held loosely around her waist. "No, Grandmother. Kearnan is a werewolf, too."

Frowning, Alesandra shook her head. "No. I would know. He doesn't smell of wolf."

"His cologne hides his scent. I didn't know myself until a couple of days ago."

Alesandra frowned. Squinting, she stepped forward, staring intently into Kearnan's face. "Gray," she muttered in a low voice. "Kearnan Gray." Then her eyes widened. "Artemis Gray. You're a son of Artemis Gray."

Behind her, Serena felt Kearnan stiffen, but she was far more interested in Alex's reaction. A look of horror appeared on his face.

Josh and Dave reacted the same way.

Even her grandmother looked troubled.

George TwoBears was the only one who didn't seem upset.

"Serena, get away from him, now," Alex demanded.

Kearnan tightened his arm. "No. She's mine. I've claimed her."

Alex shook his head. "Halfblood bastard! You have no right to her or any other female werewolf. Go back to your own kind."

Serena pushed against Kearnan's arm. "What are you talking about, Alex? Kearnan is a werewolf. I've seen him change. Grandmother, what's going on?"

Alex crossed his arms over his chest and glared at Kearnan. "Serena doesn't know, does she? You tricked her. She has the right to repudiate you." He turned his attention back to Serena. "Gray didn't tell you he's an abomination, did he? He should be out in a cage with the other wolves."

Kearnan tensed as Serena pushed against his arm again.

"His old man went feral," Alex in a triumphant tone. "He mated a wolf."

Serena frowned. Surely Alex didn't think that would upset her. "What's wrong with that?" she snapped. "Lots of werewolves choose a life in the forest. We live longer than regular wolves. Werewolves have returned from the wild when their mates died."

Alex's tone was scathing. "But, if they come back, they come back *alone*."

Alesandra's tired voice interjected. "Serena, Kearnan's mother was a wolf," she said as she leaned heavily on her cane, "a true wolf, not a werewolf."

Kearnan dropped his arm.

Trembling, Serena turned to face him. "Is this true?"

His eyes begged her to understand. "Yes."

"But…"

"My mother died when I was eight months old," he continued. "Father was devastated. He wouldn't eat, barely drank or slept. We had to do something."

"We?"

"My siblings and I. We begged him to teach us the *change*, to teach us to be human. It took years for all of us to master first the change itself and then holding this human shape. But, it kept Father alive."

"Abomination," Alex hissed from behind her. "Get away from him. He's more animal than human. Who knows what he'll do. He's dangerous, Serena."

Serena stared into Kearnan's eyes, searching for—what? *Damn it, Kearnan Gray. I finally find a man to love*—she felt herself blanch at that mental admission—*and you turn out to be something that's only talked about in whispers, a half animal half human most werewolves don't even want to admit exists.*

Serena looked back over her shoulder at Alex. Josh and Dave stood on either side of him, whispering in his ears. Alex looked confident, sure that she'd be appalled, that she'd be as prejudiced as so many other werewolves were. Werewolves who scoffed at humans for their prejudices against other humans of different ethnic backgrounds. And werewolves considered themselves superior! Bullshit.

Besides, how could anyone belittle a wolf! They were the elder brothers of werewolves. When the first werewolf had clawed its terrified way through the forest, it had been the wolves who'd saved its sanity by teaching it how to live with both its wolf and human halves. Everybody knew that. Werewolves honored wolves. Why were they so afraid of halfblood wolves who managed to master the change?

She looked back into Kearnan's face and thought back over the last three years. He was no more a monster than she or any other werewolf was.

"But you can be so gentle," she whispered in a low voice only Kearnan—and her grandmother—could hear. "For three years, I've watched you with the wolves, nursing them through illness and injuries. I've watched you patiently answer the silliest questions the children from the local schools asked about wolves. You are no abomination."

The hope that blazed in Kearnan's eyes swelled her heart.

"I love you," she whispered. Turning, she faced the others. "I'm staying here. Kearnan is no more an abomination than I am. How can you be so narrow minded? For years, our Cheyenne people were discriminated against unfairly because they were different. Now you want to do the same thing? How can you be such a hypocrite?"

Kearnan stepped forward and draped his arm around Serena's shoulders. "You heard her. She wants to stay."

Alex howled and tore at his shirt. "No, she's coming with me. She's mine! I challenge you."

Kearnan shook his head. "I don't want to fight. Serena has made her choice. Let her be."

"Never!" Alex snarled. "I mated her before you. She's mine." His body began to blur as a dark mist formed.

Serena grabbed Kearnan's arm. "No. You don't have to fight if you don't want to."

Cupping her face in his hands, he said, "Believe me, Serena, I didn't want to do this, but I have to fight now. I've been challenged in my own home."

Seizing her mouth with his, he kissed her, hard and possessively, declaring his ownership to the other males.

Alex's growl echoed throughout the room.

Removing his clothing took Kearnan only a few seconds.

Then, his form began to blur. Silvery gray mist eddied and swirled, and a gray-white wolf stood calmly where Kearnan had been.

"Kearnan, Alex, stop!" Serena yelled as the two snarling wolves faced each other.

Alesandra laid her hand on Serena' arm. "It's too late, child."

Whirling, Serena clenched Alesandra's hands. "You have to stop them, Grandmother. Kearnan's no fighter. Alex will kill him if he can."

"After you went to Alex's bed, he considered you his. In his mind, you are mated."

"Damn it, you were the one who practically pushed me into it."

Alesandra bowed her head. "The fault is mostly mine. I know. I led Alex to believe that you would stay as his mate. I was wrong. I will regret my actions for the rest of my life."

"Apology accepted," Serena snapped. "Now stop the fight."

Alesandra shook her head. "It is the way of our kind to fight for a mate. You know this. Alex believes you are his."

"But I am not Alex's mate! Yes, we had sex—once. But he did not mount me. He wasn't even my first lover, and he knows it. I will never be his mate, never!" Serena dropped her grandmother's hands and turned back to the fight. "Stupid men. Our females have always had the right to say no. We've always been free to bed whomever we want before we choose a mate. Damn it, I did not choose you, Alex."

"Alex will not acknowledge your refusal. His pride will not allow it. And, Kearnan will have to win you in battle," Alesandra said. "Even if he didn't want you for himself, Alex would still challenge Kearnan for you on principle. Many members of our pack will not accept his parentage. Your grandfather was pack Alpha. Many will believe Kearnan does not deserve you even if he does defeat Alex. If Kearnan does win, there will be those who will want you cast out of the pack for mating a halfblood."

Serena barred her teeth at her grandmother's reply. The hell with them. She didn't care what they thought. She had chosen Kearnan. That's all there was to it.

Alex and Kearnan ignored everyone else in the room. Snarls, howls, and growls echoed around the room as the two huge wolves lunged forward and crashed into each other. Bigger and bulkier, Alex chose to stand his ground. More slender and quicker, Kearnan used speed against the slower Alex. Furniture toppled and splintered when they crashed together, their teeth snapping. Tufts of fur fluttered to the floor to be followed by splatters of blood as they tore at each other's flesh. They seemed evenly matched.

Serena hugged herself with her right arm while she chewed on the knuckle of her left hand. Alex has so much more experience fighting. He'd been challenged a few times since assuming Alpha position, and he'd had to join in fights himself to stop others from trying to kill each other. Kearnan didn't have that kind of experience. He'd chosen to live his life as a man away from a pack.

Serena bit down until she drew blood when Alex slashed a deep cut in Kearnan's shoulder.

Triumphant glittered in Alex's eyes. *You will die now, abomination.*

Pain knifing though his shoulder, Kearnan snarled. He'd been holding back, afraid of what could happen if he unleashed his animal half. The human in him didn't want to hurt Alex, but this was his home. Serena was his mate.

Kearnan left the wolf in his soul free.

The blood of his wolf mother surged through his veins overpowering his humanity. Kearnan shook his head trying to clear his mind, but wolf instincts overpowered his human self. *The black Alpha challenges me for my mate. My mate! No one will take her away from me. This is my territory. I am Alpha here, and she is mine!*

Fuck you, Kearnan howled into Alex's mind and lunged for his throat.

The dark wolf shifted to meet his opponent head on, but, at the last moment, Kearnan slid to the left and slashed his opponent's ribs. Before Alex could react, Kearnan whirled and lunged low. Alex's fangs missed him completely as Kearnan's jaws locked on his enemy's left foreleg. The crack of the breaking bone reverberated throughout the room.

Mist billowed and rolled.

Bleeding profusely, Alex materialized cradling his broken arm.

Blood-flecked lips pulled back in a snarl, the silver wolf loomed over him.

His face twisted with pain and shock, Alex slid to his stomach and acknowledged Kearnan's dominance.

Silver mist swirled. Kearnan reappeared in human form, fists clenched, blood oozing from his torn flesh. Teeth barred, he snarled, "Get out." Spinning around, he strode straight to Serena, tossed her over his shoulder, and bolted up the stairs.

"Stop them," Alex commanded from between clenched teeth.

Josh and Dave looked at each other.

Face pallid, Alex pushed himself to his knees. Blood dripped from the slash on his ribs. A bone protruded from his broken arm. "You heard me."

Alesandra stepped to Alex's side and knelt. "Stay where you are, Dave. Josh, go get the first aid kit. George, I need you to help me set this bone."

"Alesandra, please."

She knelt at his side. "Enough, Alex. Serena has made her choice, and Kearnan has won her fairly."

Alex stared into her face for a moment. A groan escaped him, and he began to sag.

"Catch him, George. That's it, lay him down gently. Dave, go find me so hot water." Alesandra pointed her chin over her shoulder." I think the kitchen is that way."

As Dave disappeared into the kitchen, Josh returned with the first aid kit. "It's a good thing Alex keeps an entire medical kit in his truck," he said. "That's a nasty break."

"Stop talking and hold his shoulders, Josh. George, I'll need you to pull his arm until I'm sure the bones have slid back into place." She raised her voice. "Dave, where's my water?"

Carrying a large pot of water and a couple of towels, Dave pushed his way through the kitchen door. "Broken dishes and bones all over the place in there. Must have been a hell of a mating."

"Shut up and help Josh hold Alex down, " Alesandra commanded. "It's finished with Serena, Alex," she continued to draw his attention away from the pain. "You need to think about finding a new mate."

When both men had firm grips on his shoulders, she continued. "George, grab hold of his wrist and pull slowly until I tell you to stop. Are you ready, Alex?"

He nodded and snarled, "Stop nagging, old woman."

"The pack needs you to mate." She glanced at George. "Pull."

Alex's face paled beneath his copper skin. "Enough! I'll-find a-woman when-I'm-ready."

"Stop pulling. Hold him still."

Quickly, Alesandra washed away the blood and splinted Alex's arm. "You can let go, George. You two keep holding his shoulders. I want to stitch up the gash on his ribs after I wash it."

Alex inhaled sharply at the first jab of her needle, and gritted his teeth.

"You can't afford to wait. The women grow restless. They need an Alpha female."

Alex snarled then cursed at a particularly painful jab.

Alesandra sewed as quickly as she could. When she was finished, she washed then bandaged his chest. "You'll heal quickly enough, two weeks at the most."

Muttering about stiff joints, she pushed herself to her feet. "Josh, Dave, take him home."

"What about you?" Josh asked before Alex could.

"George and I will stay here for a few days."

"Alesandra!"

She shook her head. "No, Alex. Go home. The are plenty of unmated women there who will fall all over themselves to take care of you." Her tone softened. "You and Serena were not meant to be, Alex. Surely you realize that now."

Alex groaned as Josh and Dave helped him to his feet. "It's done," he agreed softly. He turned his face towards the door. "Take me home."

Chapter Ten

As Kearnan carried her up the stairs, primal stimuli surged through Serena's body. Her nostrils flared at the scent of Kearnan's blood—and sexual arousal. He fought for her and won. More importantly, she'd accepted him. He could have mounted her there in front of everyone, and she would have reveled in his domination.

"Mine. My mate," Kearnan growled as he kicked a door open. Once inside, he kicked the door shut, and tossed Serena onto the bed—on the other side of the room. He joined her there with one long leap, ripped the clothes from her body, and threw himself on top of her.

Blood from the gash on his shoulder smeared her breast.

Tangling his fists in her hair, he captured her mouth in a long, dominating kiss.

Lust jolted through Serena, her heat surging to answer Kearnan's aggression. This was not the playful, sexy man who'd exhausted and satiated her body the night before. This was a werewolf claiming his mate. She shuddered with anticipation—and need.

When Kearnan raised his mouth from hers, she stared into his eyes. A wolf stared back at her. He was more than a man, more than a werewolf. And she wanted him more than she'd ever wanted anything in her entire life.

"Mine," he growled. "Now." He rose, rolled her over, and lifted her to her knees.

"Oh, gods, yes." Bracing her hands high against the bed's wooden headboard, Serena spread her legs as Kearnan shoved his thigh between them, the coarse hairs of his leg rasping against the tender skin of her thigh. She moaned when his fingers brushed her swollen lips. She shifted, and he snarled, pressing his hand into the small of her back to hold her still. The muscles in her thighs shuddered when he began to thrust first one then two fingers in and out of her.

He slid his hard cock along the cleft in her behind.

Serena moaned again and bucked against his hand.

Kearnan leaned his weight on her back. "Submit," he growled into her ear. Then he nipped her shoulder.

Gasping, Serena spread her legs wider. "Yes. Fuck me, Kearnan. Fuck me hard."

He slid his fingers out of her and pinched her clit.

She bucked back against him again, rotating her ass against his cock. "Please…"

Panting harshly, Kearnan grabbed her hips, pushed her forward, and thrust a thigh between her legs, spreading them even farther apart. He held her still, positioning her for his first thrust. "Mine," he snarled. "My mate."

Serena arched her back, anticipating, longing for the hard thrust that would bury his cock inside of her. "Now, Kearnan, please, hard, fuck me hard."

Pressing a hand into the small of her back to make her arch even more, Kearnan rammed his cock into her, thrusting his hips in short jabs to seat it as deeply as he could.

Serena felt herself oozing around him. She ground her ass against his hips shuddering as his wiry pubic hairs caressed the soft skin of her behind. She pushed back harder, helping Kearnan bury his cock even deeper inside of her, deeper than he'd ever been before.

Serena shuddered as her body stretched and adjusted itself around him. She had never felt so stretched, so full, so hot, as if every inch of his cock was burning inside of her. Her clit pulsated. She needed to come.

"Gods, you're so hard."

Snarling, Kearnan curled over her back, and bit down on her shoulder, using his powerful jaws to immobilize her. He covered her left hand with his, lacing his fingers through hers. Then he began pumping his hips.

Serena keened her pleasure. Kearnan's right hand slid up her stomach and ribcage to knead her breast. Her nipples seared to achingly pleasurable points.

He released her shoulder and lifted his head. "Mine. My mate," he hissed in her ear. "Only mine." His teeth clamped onto her shoulder again.

"Yours, only yours," Serena moaned in answer.

Kearnan thrust harder, his pistoning hips driving her towards the headboard, lifting her knees until she was almost vertically flat against the high oak headboard of his antique bed.

Serena reveled in Kearnan's dominate mating as new sensations exploded throughout her body, sensations she'd only heard about from mated female werewolves. Kearnan's teeth were clamped on her shoulder holding her immobile to his will. This was how a werewolf claimed his mate.

Kearnan used his greater strength to trap Serena between him and the bed's headboard and continued to ram his hips against her ass, to plunge his cock into her as deeply as he could. She was his. He had shed blood for her, defeated an enemy for her. Her thighs were spread and her ass was rubbing against his hips. His balls were on fire, and his cock felt ready to explode, but he fought his orgasm and continued to pound into Serena. She was his, his alone. No other werewolf would ever mate her again. He would brand her with his scent and seed so every werewolf in the world would recognize her as his, including Serena herself.

"I can't wait," Serena moaned. "I'm going to come."

Kearnan slammed himself into to her harder. "You—are—mine!"

Serena froze against him. "Yours, Kearnan. My mate." She threw her head back and howled as her orgasm ripped through her body.

Kearnan's last few thrusts lifted Serena off the bed. Then his deeper howled joined hers, and he collapsed against her, only the sound of their harsh breathing breaking the silence.

Panting, Kearnan braced both hands on the headboard of his bed to take some of his weight off of Serena's back and rested his forehead on her shoulder. Once he caught his breath, he pushed himself away and collapsed on the bed, his arm thrown over his eyes.

Never had sex been so good.

Never had he been so violent.

Never had he felt so afraid of himself.

For years he'd struggled to control his animal side, to keep the untamed instincts and urges that boiled through his blood under control. He'd chosen a human life over that of a wolf. He would not act like an animal. Yet, the moment Serena had been threatened, he'd fought with the intent to rip out another man's throat. And, after he'd defeated his rival, he'd taken Serena to his bed and mounted her like she was some kind of animal.

Gods, what was he becoming?

Sighing contentedly, Serena slid down to his side and snuggled against him.

Kearnan drew away. "I'm sorry."

Her voice was surprised. "Sorry? Why?"

He turned his head away, his arm still over his eyes. "For the way I treated you. My behavior was inexcusable. It won't happen again."

Her chuckle was deep and throaty. "Why not?"

"Because you won't be here."

Serena pushed away from his back and sat up. "What!"

Kearnan still refused to look at her. "Damn it, Serena, all I've ever heard is that my mother was a wolf, an animal, that I was less than everyone else, that I couldn't be trusted with anyone's daughter because I might go feral on her. I've spent most of my life fighting to keep the wolf half, the animal half, of me under control, to protect those around me. Today, I completely lost control. I could have killed Alex. I almost did. I can't let it happen again."

"But you didn't kill him. You stopped."

"This time. And what about how I treated you? I couldn't have stopped fucking you if I'd had to. I was totally out of control."

Chuckling, Serena leaned against him and rubbed her breasts against his back. "Can we do it again?"

Lowering his arm, Kearnan turned to face her. "Do it again? For Christ's sake, my lust was so strong, all I could think of was mounting you, of overpowering you until whether you accepted my dominance or not. I didn't care if you liked what I was doing, if I was hurting you, if you didn't want me. I was only thinking of myself. Damn it, Serena, that's rape."

Her voice piqued, she jerked away. " You're a werewolf, Kearnan. You fought off a challenger who wanted me. What's more, I'm in heat. You acted exactly how you were supposed to act. Besides, I'm not complaining. I liked it. I would have liked it if you had mounted me in front of everyone to prove your claim. But you didn't to that. You care enough about me to bring me up here where we could be alone, where no one else would see me submit to you."

Kearnan shook his head. "That's not the point. If I can attack you like this now, what will I do next time? I could hurt you. No. I won't allow that to happen. It will be better if you leave."

The bed heaved as she rolled off the other side. "Leave? You want me to leave? After chaining me to the bed and fucking the daylights out of me for almost two days, you want me to leave! You ass. You self-centered, manipulative fuckhead. Go to hell."

Dark mist swirled, and a black wolf sprang over the bed and sprinted out of the room—without opening the door. It split down the center. Half lay splintered on the floor. The rest sagged from the top hinge.

Kearnan rolled over and stared out the window. "Without you, Serena, I'm in hell all ready."

Alesandra was climbing the staircase when Serena bolted past her.

"Serena!"

The wolf ignored her and leaped through the storm door, leaving the tattered screen dangling behind her.

Alesandra sighed and muttered. "She always runs away."

Alesandra continued up the stairway and down the hall, stopping in front of the shattered door. Kearnan Gray reclined on the bed, his back facing her.

Nice ass, she thought to herself as she stepped into the room. "What have you done to my granddaughter?"

He didn't bother to roll over. "Told her something she didn't want to hear."

Alesandra settled into an overstuffed chair. "Oh, and what was that."

"The truth."

"She knew the truth about your ancestry before she declared her willingness to become your mate. What other truths are there?"

Kearnan rolled over and sat up. Glaring at Alesandra, he pushed himself off the bed. He stood before, making no move to cover himself.

Alesandra's gaze roamed down Kearnan's body to his crotch. "You're not saying Serena was dissatisfied with the sex? You're hung well enough to satisfy any woman."

Kearnan snorted with sour laughter. "Can an abomination such as I satisfy any woman? I covered your granddaughter like she was an animal, old woman. I bit her. I clamped her shoulder in my jaws to keep her from struggling against me, to hold her still while I mated her. It was more rape than love. What woman would want to be treated like that?"

Alesandra shook her head. "What fool raised you?"

Nostrils flaring, Kearnan stepped forward. "My father…"

"Your father was a man heart-broken over the loss of his mate. You're right. If you and your sibs hadn't demanded that he teach you the change, he would have sought the dark path. But, Artemis Gray was a werewolf who enjoyed sex and celebrated it to the fullest of his senses before he chose to stay with your mother. He did not tell you to control your passions by hiding behind your humanity."

Kearnan stared at Alesandra. "How do you know…"

Her smile interrupted him. "I was young once, too. And, like Serena, I was entirely too willful. My lovers were wide and varied before I mated her grandfather. Your father and I spent a full moon together once. I still have scars from his teeth."

"But…"

"Whoever told you to control the wolf in you to the extent that you had to keep your emotions under control in a full werewolf mating was a fool—or afraid to lose you."

Kearnan's narrowed eyes confirmed her hunch.

Alesandra sniffed. "A woman. I should have known. Who was she?"

Hands clenched, Kearnan walked to the door and wrenched what was left of it from its hinges. He tossed it on top of the half already on the floor and turned back to Alesandra. "Once we were all able to hold our human forms fairly consistently, Father took us to his pack. It never occurred to any of us that so many of our father's people would hate us.

The vote to cast us out was close. A last minute plea by my father's mother swayed just enough votes in our favor."

"So you were pack yet not pack."

"It wasn't so bad as long as my grandmother was alive. She held a great deal of power and respect within the pack. My brothers and I managed to meet a few younger males willing to be our friends. My sisters seemed to fare better. There were always young females about. Of course, all of them were warned to stay away from my brothers and me."

Alesandra snorted. "That's like telling a child not to eat the candy lying in plain sight on the table."

Kearnan nodded.

"Which one ruined you?"

He shook his head. "Not one of the girls. Not me, Garth. The sad thing is, she really loved him. Her parents sent her away to another pack."

"None of your sisters' friends were interested in you?

Kearnan shrugged. "They may have been. I wasn't interested in them." He looked full into Alesandra's face for the first time. "No, there was an older woman, a widow who I wanted. And she returned my interest. She was in heat the first time I met her. She was hot and willing. I spent more time in her bed than in my own, even after her heat was over. Then my grandmother died."

After a bitter laugh, Kearnan continued. "Suddenly, my sisters' friends stopped coming around. More and more pack members began shunning us."

"And your widow?"

"Told me I was a stinking animal. She said she'd done her best to teach me how to be a man and not a beast in bed, but I was too rough, too interested in only my own pleasure. No woman, even a werewolf, would ever want me in her bed because I didn't care how much I hurt them as long as I was satisfied. She said all that she got from me were bites and bruises without satisfaction."

"She doesn't deserve to be called a bitch."

Kearnan nodded. "True, but the bruises and bite marks I gave her were real. That day I swore I'd never treat a woman like that again."

"She threatened to bring complaint against you to the pack Alpha if you said anything to anyone, didn't she?" Alesandra said in a thoughtful voice.

When Kearnan nodded his head, Alesandra pounded her cane against the floor and snarled, "Evil woman. All you had to do was ask a mature male, and you would have learned the truth. The witch only wanted to ruin your life, and she almost did."

Kearnan glared at her. "We left shortly after that. Father took us to New York, away from pack life so we could learn to be completely human—as much as a werewolf can. With his sensitive nose, he was able to get a job with a small men's cologne manufacturer, and, well, you know the rest of the story."

"He introduced a new line of men's cologne and is making a fortune," Alesandra said dryly.

Kearnan nodded. "Anyway, from then on, we were raised among humans. A few werewolves passed through our lives now and then, but for my brothers and me, sex was something we learned about from our human friends. Father made it clear bruising and biting our lovers was not acceptable behavior. He told us to keep a leash on the wolf side of us unless we had a nonhuman lover, so we learned to control ourselves. Serena is the first nonhuman I've been with since we lived with the pack. Old habits die hard. Half of me was demanding that I fuck her into submission, and the other half was condemning me for wanting to do it."

Sighing, Alesandra said, "Such a confusing life you've led." Pushing herself to her feet, she walked across the room until she stood before him. "Kearnan, your mother may have been a wolf, and there are those of our kind who will always be prejudiced against you. But, the blood of wolves flows through all our veins—just to a lesser extent than yours. That woman lied to you. The extra wolf blood you carry will ensure you never hurt Serena. You're the expert on wolves. Have you ever known even the most ferocious male to hurt his mate even during mating?"

Frowning, Kearnan stared at Alesandra.

"Just think about it, Kearnan," she continued. "However out-of-control and violent you believed yourself to be, Serena would have fought if she didn't like what you were doing to her. There is no rape in the animal kingdom. When in heat, a female werewolf craves a wild mating. To normal humans, it appears brutal, but to us it's a necessity. Follow your instincts. They'll never lie to you."

"Damn fucking Clarisse. If I ever get my hands on her," Kearnan said more to himself than to Alesandra. He began to pace. Then he stopped and stared at the broken door. "I told Serena to leave."

Alesandra rolled her eyes. "Youth. What a waste on the young. Where would she have gone?"

Kearnan's shoulders slumped. "For all I know, she left for good."

Alesandra smiled and shook her head. "She's mated you now. She will not leave."

A hopeful smile spread across Kearnan's lips. "Blossom and Storm have four month old cubs. She spends a lot of time with them."

Alesandra nodded. "Then that's where she'll be."

As Kearnan started towards the door, she laid a hand on his arm. "She must not change again. Changing could cause her to abort if the child has settled into her womb."

Kearnan stopped abruptly. "Child?"

Alesandra chuckled. "Only aconite tea will keep a female werewolf from becoming pregnant if she's mated during her "wolf heat."

"Aconite?"

"Wolfsbane," Alesandra answered in an exasperated voice. "I thought you were and expert on wolves."

"I know what aconite is," Kearnan replied. "How can you possibly know if Serena is pregnant?"

Alesandra chuckled. "I believe I heard her say that you chained her to the bed and fucked the daylights out of her."

Kearnan flushed. Werewolves had excellent hearing. Hell, with as loud as Serena was shouting when he told her to leave, the wolves themselves probably heard her.

"Where's Alex?" he asked in a neutral tone.

"Gone, licking his wounds and his pride. Maybe now he will see to his duties as Alpha and quit dwelling on Serena, that is unless you and Serena wish to return with us. You have won the right to be Alpha."

Kearnan shook his head. "I—we belong here."

Alesandra smiled. "Then go tell her that."

As Kearnan turned to leave the room, the boom of a shotgun blast reverberated through the house.

Chapter Eleven

ꟾ

In wolf form, Kearnan hurtled across the room and out the door. He plunged down the staircase. His claws clicked and scraped as he skidded across the slippery hardwood floor of the living room. In the seconds it took him to reach the front door, another shotgun blast rolled through the house. The door that lost its screen from Serena's passage was torn completely off its hinges as Kearnan exploded through it. At this moment, he had no doubts about himself. His mate was in danger. If anyone had hurt her, he'd rip out his throat.

Eyes tearing from the force of the wind caused by his speed, Kearnan sprinted across the small lawn and down the hill towards the laboratory. He sprang past the out buildings and tore down the rutted track that lay between the wolf enclosures. The shotgun blast had come from the northernmost corner of the enclosures—the enclosure where Blossom had dug her den and birthed her cubs. He returned to his human form only long enough to unlatch the gate leading Blossom's enclosure. Serena had definitely been here not long ago. Her scent lingered on the bushes bordering the path.

Nostrils flared, Kearnan lifted his head and searched the breeze. That way, north. Serena was at Blossom's den, just as he'd thought. Mist swirled as he changed, and the gray wolf sprang north towards the woman he loved.

When the first shotgun blast exploded not far from her, Serena chased the wolf cubs into their den. When the pellets from the second blast raked through the leaves above her head, she dove behind a boulder.

Raucous laughter drifted to her with the breeze.

"Think we hit any of them wolves, Fred?"

"Don't know, Daryl. I thought I saw something moving in the mountain laurel."

Serena peered around the rock and started to shake. One of her worst nightmares had come true. The Hadley brothers stood in a clearing on the other side of the chain link fence. She leaned back against the boulder. *Oh shit! And I'm naked. Rape is a sporting event to them. Maybe, if I'm lucky, they'll go away.*

She clapped her hands over her ears as another round of shotgun pellets raked the underbrush to her right. Thankfully the wolf den was on the other side.

Calm down, Serena, there's an eight-foot chain link fence between them and you. They might be able to shoot you, but they won't be able to touch you.

The cub's whimpering grew louder.

Serena closed her eyes and sent a mental command to both the cubs cowering in the den and their parents who were sprinting frantically back to the den. *Stay where you are. I'll take care of this. No one will hurt the cubs.*

"Hey, Fred. Do ya think we can skin one of them wolves if we shoot it? I always wanted ta hang a wolf skin on the wall.

One of their skins? That son of a bitch. Over my dead body will one of those assholes hang anything from a wolf on his wall.

"You stupid assholes!" Serena yelled as she sprang to her feet and stepped from behind the boulder. "What do you think you're doing?" She stood legs spread, feet planted firmly, her hands fisted on her hips, and glared at the two men.

The breeze shifted, and the scent of sour human sweat and stale alcohol wafted towards her. Gagging, she turned her face away.

Low, fearful whines from the wolf den drew her attention.

Stay where you are babies. Mama and Papa are fine, and I'll keep you safe.

Blossom's cubs huddled inside their den, Serena's mental command keeping them still.

Serena tilted her head at the slight sound of rustling brush and caught the scent of female wolf. Blossom. That meant Storm was also nearby. Thank the gods that neither had been hit by the initial shotgun blasts, but Blossom was becoming more and more fretful about the safety of her cubs.

I won't let anything happen to them, Blossom. I'll get these monsters away from your cubs.

The two men pointed their shotguns at her.

"Lookie, Fred, she's naked." Daryl Hadley drooled, licked the slobber from his lips, then drooled more. His dirty-blonde hair hung in clumps to his shoulders. His right eyelid drooped over watery, blue eyes. He was missing two of his front teeth.

A mere inch shorter and maybe twenty pounds lighter than Daryl, Fred was dressed in dirty camouflage pants tucked into hunting boots and a ratty, flannel shirt. He had all of his teeth, but they stained brown from the tobacco wad constantly in his mouth. His eyes were the same pale blue, but the look in them was meaner. Unlike Daryl, Fred had some intelligence.

Both men's gazes traveled the length of her body more than once. Daryl then riveted his gaze on her breasts while Fred stared at the dark curls between her legs. They shuffled their feet, shifting to accommodate the bulges at the front of their jeans.

"I wanna fuck her, Fred," Daryl mumbled through his spittle. "I wanna fuck her good."

Fred motioned with his gun. "Get over here, girl."

Shaking her head, Serena threw up her hands. *I can do this. I can get them away from the cubs.* "Idiot. Even if I were so inclined to come anywhere near your rancid bodies, and believe me I'm not, there's a chain-link fence between us. No gate."

Daryl shifted his shotgun to one arm and jerked at the button on his jeans. "Make her come here, Fred. My dick hurts something fierce. I can fuck her through the fence."

"Shut up," Fred snapped, his eyes never leaving Serena. "Where's the gate?"

She crossed her arms under her breasts, lifting and squeezing them together. "The main gate of each compound is at the center of the preserve. That's down by the house."

Her nipples pebbled from the cool air.

Both men shifted their gazes to her breasts.

Daryl shifted from foot to foot and whined, "How are we going to get her, Fred?" His jeans were sagging around his hips.

Serena kept her tone light. "There's a small auxiliary gate about a quarter of a mile from here."

Daryl took a step forward, but Fred stopped him. "Why you telling us about the gate?"

Serena contemplated Fred Hadley. *This one isn't as dumb as he looks. The truth is probably the best answer. He'll figure he can come shoot the wolves another time.* "To get you away from the wolves," she answered. "I don't want you shooting at them."

"How do you know we won't still shoot you?" Fred continued in a suspicious voice.

"Because that would be murder, and you aren't murders. You're just a couple of good old boys trying to make your community a safer place. Besides, I've been watching you two. Staying out here on the preserve most of the time gets lonely sometimes, but I don't like going into town. You guys like the woods and nature. We probably have a lot in common."

As Serena talked, Daryl set the butt of his shotgun on the ground and shoved his free hand down the front of his jeans. His hand began to move up and down. An idiotic grin on his face, he said, "See, Fred. She ain't so stuck up. She did smile at me that time in town. I was right. I told you so."

Fred addressed his answer to Serena, obviously still suspicious. "Then how come you would never talk to us when you saw us? How come you was always so uppity, like we wasn't good enough for you?"

Serena unclasped her arms and shrugged.

Her breasts jiggled.

"My boss. He threatened to fire all of us if we were friendly towards you. He's afraid you'll convince the rest of the town to make him get rid of the wolves."

Fred puffed out his chest. "Son of a bitch should be afraid of us. Only a matter of time till the rest of the people around here sees things our way." His eyes slipped down to Serena's crotch again. "What you doing out here naked?"

Serena shifted her feet. Her breasts jiggled again. "My boss likes to play games."

Daryl's hand moved faster. His gaze was glued to her chest.

Doubt still on his face, Fred said, "And you let him? Didn't think women nowadays let their bosses get away with fucking them around, all that sexual harassment stuff."

Serena smiled. "He pays me $500 bucks. Puts it down as hazard pay cause I'm in the wolf enclosures with the wolves."

Fred grunted. "$500 bucks to fuck in the woods? Didn't know you could make that much money raising wolves."

Serena just shrugged.

Her breasts bounced.

Daryl groaned and then grunted. He began to pant.

Fred ignored his brother. "How come you're offering to fuck us both?"

"He'll pay me double to do both of you while he watches. He'll probably pay you too."

Fred jerked his head up. Greed oozed into his voice. "He'll pay us to fuck you?"

"Sure. Any of his employees willing to do kinky sex get paid extra. Like I said, he likes to watch."

Daryl's breath was now labored. Inside his jeans, his hand moved faster. "Make her spread her legs wider, Fred."

Fred lowered his shotgun and punched Daryl in the arm. "Stop it. "You'll blow your whole load before you even stick her. You know you won't be able to get it up right away again."

Knocked off balance by his brother's blow, Daryl staggered, dropped his gun, and used both hands to grab onto a tree to keep from falling. Once he regained his balance, he grabbed his shotgun and pointed at Serena's stomach. The glare he sent her was chilling. "Where's the gate, bitch?"

Serena swallowed and glanced at Fred.

He was grinning. "Don't worry, honey. Daryl likes cornholing, but it don't take him no time to come. You can get down on your hands and knees so Daryl can stick you in your ass doggy style, or him and me can squeeze you between us. Then I can ram your cunt while Daryl pokes your ass. How much will your boss pay to see that?"

"Shut up, Fred." Daryl poked his shotgun to the left. "Show me where the gate is, bitch. And don't try nothing funny. I can still fuck you if I shoot you in the leg. A little blood don't bother me none."

"Better get movin', honey. When Daryl is this horny, he can get down right mean. Sometimes he likes to use other stuff before he sticks his dick in a woman."

Serena shivered. She'd always thought Fred Hadley controlled his little brother. Maybe she was wrong. Trying to escape by diving into the undergrowth, even with her werewolf speed was out of the question. The Hadleys were just on the other side of the fence. Two shotgun blasts from this range would inflict damage before even the fastest werewolf could get out of the way.

Glancing over her shoulder, Serena spied Blossom duck into her den. As soon as she and the two men were out of sight, the wolves would take their cubs toward the center of the preserve, towards the house where they would all be safe.

Serena peeked at the Hadleys from beneath her eyelashes.

Both had their shotguns trained on her.

Both were grinning maniacally.

"Get moving."

Serena glanced around once more. Where the hell was Kearnan? She was his mate. He better get his ass out here. She motioned to her left. "Sure, this way."

As they walked, she on her side of the fence they on theirs, the normal sounds of the forest died. Birds didn't chirp. Squirrels didn't chatter. Not even a breeze rustled the leaves. The only sound was the noisy tramping of the Hadley brothers' passage as they tripped, shoved, and cursed their way through the underbrush.

Then, the howl of a hunting wolf shattered the silence.

Serena turned her face away from the Hadley brothers and grinned. Kearnan was coming.

Chapter Twelve

ഀ

Howls erupted all over the preserve as the wolves answered Kearnan.

Daryl tripped over an exposed root. "Fred, you got extra shells?"

"Forget them wolves. None of them are close," Fred answered. "Are they?" he continued to Serena.

She shook her head. "After the shots you fired, the wolves are all as far away as they can get."

"What are they howling about?"

"The gunshots. They're talking to each other, making sure none of them have been shot."

"You talk about them like they're human," Fred said. He sounded suspicious again.

Think fast, Serena. Fred's starting to think again. Better jiggle your boobs some more or wiggle your ass. Get his thoughts back to his dick. "Ouch!" she exclaimed.

"What?"

"Branch hit me." She cupped her breast in her left hand and rubbed her nipple with her right.

Fred's Adam's apple bobbed as he swallowed. He gagged, coughed, and spit out his tobacco wad.

Turning her head to hide her grin, Serena stepped over a small log. Fred was thinking with his dick again.

As she walked, Serena's mind whirled. Kearnan was coming. She frowned. Would he do something stupid like try to take on two men with guns? She muttered a curse under her breath. Of course, he would. He was male. Now she was going to have to rescue the both of them somehow. Unless... A thick stand of pines grew before her. She just had to keep the Hadleys from realizing they wouldn't be able to see her once they were all inside the pines.

Outside the fence, the Hadley brothers kept pace with her, forcing their way through sometimes dense undergrowth. One of them always had a shotgun pointed at her. Sweat stained the fronts, backs, and underarms of both men's flannel shirts.

The breeze shifted, carrying their rank stench to Serena. She cursed under her breath.

"Now what's the matter?" Fred growled.

"I stepped on another stone." *If they get any closer, I'll puke. When was the last time either one of them bathed?*

"How much further is that gate, bitch?"

"Another hundred yards or so. It's right through this stand of pines." She pretended to stumble. "Ouch! I think I stepped on a thorn." Turning her back on them, Serena bent over, giving the men a clear view of her behind.

"Look at her ass," Daryl moaned. "An her cunt. Look at how red it is."

Serena heard lips smacking.

"Get going, girl. An we ain't waiting for yer boss. Son of a bitch can pay us to watch another time."

Straightening, Serena waved her hand and gestured forward. "The gate is on the other side of this stand of pine trees." Pushing the fragrant, supple boughs out of her way, she disappeared into the pines.

When the Hadley brothers forced their way to the other side of the pines, Serena was nowhere to be seen. Neither was a gate.

Daryl pushed his belly up against the fence, swinging his head from right to left. "Hey, where'd she go?"

Fred stared through the fence. Then he threw his hat to the ground. "Son of a bitch. Fuckin' whore tricked us."

When the hand clamped over Serena's mouth, she bit it.

"It's me, damn it," Kearnan growled in her ear as he wrapped his arm around her waist and pulled her back against his naked body.

After he dropped his hand from her mouth, Serena hissed, "Why didn't you come in from upwind? I'd have known you were here."

The crisp hairs on his legs teased the backs of her thighs.

"Because I didn't know what I was going to find. I just got here as quickly as I could. When I saw where you were leading them, I slipped into the pines and waited. What the hell do you think you're doing letting them see you naked? You know what those two are like, what they'll do to you if they ever get their hands on you."

"What else was I supposed to do?" Serena hissed. "They were going to keep shooting into the underbrush until they hit something. I knew they couldn't get through the fence; and, once they got a look at me naked, I could talk them into following me anywhere. Besides, I knew you'd come."

Kearnan nipped the back of her neck. "That sure of me, are you? What if you had reached the gate before I got here?"

Serena shivered. "I'd have thought of something, and there's a lock on the gate."

"They could have shot it off," he murmured against her shoulder.

She pushed at the arm wrapped around her waist. "Damn it, what else was I supposed to do?"

"Shhhhhh. I'm sorry. I know you were trying to save the cubs." Kearnan tightened his arm around her waist. "So, your boss likes to watch you having sex?"

"You heard that?"

"I heard everything. And I do enjoy watching you have sex—alone. If another man ever touches you, he's dead. You're mine." He caressed her side then cupped her breast, flicking her nipple with his thumb. After squeezing her breast gently, he slid his hand down her ribcage and caressed her stomach. "Did you drink any aconite tea before you came up to the house?"

"Aconite tea, no why… Oh."

Kearnan wrapped his other arm around Serena and hugged her. "Do you mind?"

A baby. I never thought… Serena leaned back against Kearnan, absorbing his warmth and his strength. "No. No I don't."

Kearnan kissed the side of her neck. "I'm glad. I love you, Serena."

Even the two armed men only a few hundred yards away didn't stop the shiver of anticipation from skipping down her spine as Kearnan's warm breath caressed her neck.

His cock stirred against her ass.

A shotgun blasted off to their right.

His voice low, Kearnan cursed. "Later, sweet." He dragged his tongue down the side of Serena's neck and along her shoulder.

After she shivered, he dropped his arm from her waist and gently pushed her away.

Kearnan turned his head towards the fence. His voice hardened. "I've tolerated those two long enough."

Serena's stomach rolled. "What are you going to do?"

"Get rid of them once and for all."

She grabbed his arm. "You can't. When their mangled bodies are found, the authorities will come straight here, and the wolves, not you, will suffer."

Kearnan jerked his arm free. "The bodies won't be found."

Screams erupted on the other side of the pine thicket.

"Don't you dare change," Kearnan commanded. Silvery mist formed and floated and floated through the pines.

"Don't change," Serena muttered. "As if I'd purposely take a chance on hurting the baby. I can get there faster on two legs anyhow."

A shotgun thundered again.

Shoving pine branches out of her way Serena sprinted the last few feet. Once clear of the trees, she slid to a stop beside Kearnan.

He stood ten feet from the fence, fists planted on his hips.

On the other side, the Hadley brothers were battling a grizzly bear. With one swing of its paw, the bear knocked Daryl's shotgun from his hand. It slammed into the chain link fence, jamming itself halfway through.

Fred aimed his gun at the bear only to have it knocked to the side.

Kearnan shoved Serena to the ground and covered her body with his as buckshot flew above their heads. "Buckshot. They were going to shoot the wolves with buckshot so they'd suffer," he growled and pushed himself to his feet. "I'll rip out their hearts."

Serena tackled him by wrapping her arms around his knees. "Not even you can fight that bear."

Fred screamed.

Kearnan and Serena jerked their attention back to the men and bear.

The bear had both men in front of him, his paws on their necks. Then it slammed their heads together. Daryl and Fred dropped to the ground and lay still.

Brown mist swirled, and George TwoBears stood before them.

"A werebear," Serena sputtered. "You're a werebear."

George nodded through the fence. "Yes."

She gawked. "Yes? That's all you have to say?"

"Your grandmother has called the police. Perhaps it is best if I take them back to the house and tie them up before they regain consciousness." With those words, he grabbed both men and hefted one onto each shoulder. "How far to the gate?"

Kearnan paced along the inside of the fence. "This way. Only another hundred yards. Do you want any help?"

"No."

George trailed Kearnan along the outside of the fence until they reached the gate. There, Kearnan wrenched the lock from it's bracket. "I'll get another one."

George stepped through the gate and readjusted his load. Then he strode away towards the house.

Kearnan raked his fingers through his hair and stared after George TwoBears. He'd been so intent on Serena and Alex's challenge, he hadn't paid any attention to the man at Alesandra's side. Propping his hands on his hips, Kearnan watched TwoBears progress until he disappeared through some dense brush.

He never saw Serena launch herself at him. Wrapping her arms around his waist, she tackled him, tumbling him over. When they finally stopped rolling, Kearnan was flat on his back. Serena straddled his waist with her knees and lower legs hugging the sides of his body. Her hands pressed his shoulders to the ground as she glared down at him.

"Damn it, Serena, you could have hurt yourself."

She lifted her hand and stabbed a finger into his chest. "Just shut up and listen to me, Dr. Kearnan Gray. I want you to understand something just in case you get into another funk about having a wolf for a mother. I'm not leaving. You claimed me, and I agreed to your claim, so you're stuck with me. I don't give a damn about who your mother was or how much wolf you have in you."

"Serena…"

She leaned closer until her face was only inches from his. "Don't interrupt. I'm a werewolf. You can't hurt me during mating. Not only am I strong enough to handle it, I wouldn't let you do anything I didn't enjoy. No matter how feral you get, I could stop you."

One quick twist and Serena was flat on her back. Kearnan settled himself on her, cradled his erection against the soft curls of her pubis, and smiled down at her. He dipped his head and nipped her neck. "Now what are you going to do?"

Her chuckle was low as she danced the fingers of her left hand down his spine. When she wrapped her right arm around his neck and pulled his mouth down to hers, Kearnan didn't fight her.

He covered her mouth, sighing, as Serena's tongue mated with his.

Her left hand caressed his ass then slid along his hip.

Kearnan shifted and spread his legs wider when she slipped her hand between them. With a contented growl, he shifted more when she slid her fingers around his cock and pumped him twice.

When she dug her nails into his cock, he yanked his mouth from hers.

"Serena!"

She grinned. "So you could do anything to me, huh? Get off." She dug her nails in a little deeper.

Eyes narrowed, Kearnan rolled off her, content for the moment to see what game she played.

Serena followed, straddling him again. This time, though, she sat further back on his hips, his cock between her thighs. Before he could comment, she slid back his legs, dipped her head, and sucked him into her mouth.

"Jesus," he gasped as his back arched and he shoved his cock deeper into her mouth. He grasped her head with both hands and began to pump. The hell with being gentle.

Serena opened her mouth wider and relaxed her throat muscles. She had him just where she wanted him.

Kearnan's breath came faster. He pumped harder.

Serena's nipples ached, and she could feel moisture trickling down the inside of her thighs. But, she had a point to prove. Bracing her hands against his hips, she waited until he'd pulled his cock most of the way out of her mouth and clamped her teeth around the head.

Kearnan froze and snarled. *That hurt!* "No games, Serena. Submit."

"No," she mumbled, her mouth full of his cock.

Trembling with frustration and anger, Kearnan released her head. "You bitch."

Serena immediately opened her mouth.

Pulling himself free with a curse, Kearnan tackled Serena, dropping the full weight of his body on top of her. "I'm tired of your games, Serena," he snarled. "You want me, you take me as I am."

She raised her chin and stared into his eyes. "Are you going to beat me?"

Shock replaced his anger. "What?"

"Are you going to beat me? Or rape me?"

Anger returned. "I do not beat or rape women."

"Then why," she continued in a gentler voice, "do you think you could ever hurt me? I certainly just provoked you enough. At least three members of my old pack would have backhanded me off their cocks if I had done that to them."

Head lowered, stormy gray eyes unblinking, Kearnan stared down into her face.

Her voice was quiet. "I did a lot of thinking before the Hadley brothers started shooting. The fact that your mother was a wolf makes you better than normal werewolves."

Kearnan shifted some weight off of her and cocked an eyebrow. "Really?"

Serena's temper began to flare. *Why did men have to be so damn obtuse?* "Damn it, Kearnan, you've been studying wolves for how many years now? Have you ever seen a mated pair separate? Either the male or female hurt each other?"

An arrogant expression on his face, Kearnan stared at her. "No."

"Well, then, what the hell is your problem with your heritage? Werewolves are mostly human, with human faults. We make a big deal about lifetime bonds with our mates, but there are werewolves who are unfaithful, who shame their mates by having sex with others. Males who beat their wives or children. Mothers who run out on their children. Wolves don't do that. Your wolf mother's blood is a good thing, Kearnan. I'll be proud of any children we have, knowing that they'll have a stronger pack instinct than many "pure blooded" werewolves."

The corners of his mouth twitched. "So going down on me was just to prove a point?"

Serena grinned, "Well, I do enjoy sucking on your cock, but I had to prove you'd never hurt me."

Kearnan shifted more of his weight from Serena. She'd certainly managed to prove her point. He'd never hurt her. How had he managed to get so lucky? Two days ago she was trying to run away from him. Now he couldn't drive her away. Smiling, he pushed himself to his feet and held out his hand.

Serena ignored it and launched herself against his chest.

Kearnan wrapped his arms around her and hugged her tight. "I'm glad I chained you to the bed."

She pushed free and sank to her knees before him. One kiss had his cock fully erect. She looked up into his eyes. "So am I."

Chapter Thirteen

ℰ𝒪

Leaning back in his chair, Kearnan watched as Serena rocked back and forth, cooing gently to the baby cuddled in her arms. Fingers laced behind his head, he smiled as she pulled her tee shirt up and guided their daughter's mouth to her distended nipple. Hand fisted against her mother's breast, Morgan sucked noisily.

Kearnan felt his cock stir. Serena's breasts were larger now that they were full of milk for the baby. Early in her pregnancy, when her breasts had first filled out, he'd been delighted and spent many enjoyable hours kissing and sucking on them. And now that Morgan was born and nursing, he found Serena's breasts even more fascinating.

Her nipples fascinated him more than any other woman's ever had. A warm tan color, they were always hard and pebbled now. Of course, that was because of Morgan nursing, but Serena's breasts didn't just supply nourishment for their daughter. They also provided Kearnan enough sexual stimulation to keep him hard and aching for hours.

With a yawn, the baby let go of her mother's nipple and drifted into sleep.

Sighing contentedly, Serena rose from her rocking chair and laid the baby in her cradle. Then she turned back to Kearnan.

His groin tightened.

Her shirt was still pushed up over her breast.

As Kearnan watched, a drop of milk welled from the exposed nipple.

Grinning, Serena cupped her breast. "You're staring at my nipples again. Are you thirsty too?"

Leaning forward, Kearnan grabbed her waist and pulled her between his legs. His hands slid up her sides and pushed her shirt up over both breasts. When the drop of milk fell from Serena's breast, he caught it on his tongue.

Serena wrapped her arms around Kearnan's head and hugged him. He nuzzled her breast and excitement shot through her.

His hands began to knead her behind.

Serena shivered, but there was no time for this now.

"You have to feed the wolves, my love," she breathed into his hair.

He slid his hands down to her hips, tilted his head back, and stared into her eyes. "I know. I just couldn't resist, especially when you tease me the way you do."

"But you like to be teased."

Kearnan grinned. "No, you like what I do to you when you tease me."

Serena chuckled and cupped his face between her hands. "Have I told you how much I love you today?"

"Only once," Kearnan answered as he raised his lips to hers.

Some moments later, Serena pulled away. As always, his mouth drew the soul from her body. Resting her forehead against Kearnan's, she said, "You really have to go. The cubs need to be fed, or they'll gnaw their way through the fence."

With a sigh that was half moan half chuckle, Kearnan released Serena's hips. After she stepped back, he rose. The bulge in the front of his jeans was quite noticeable.

Serena grinned. "I could take care of that for you."

He grinned back. "Later, I'll make you eat your words. But for now, you're right. Those wolf cubs will start gnawing on the fence if I don't feed them."

After a quick kiss on her forehead, Kearnan leaped from the porch and headed towards the shed where the dog food was stored.

Settling back onto her rocking chair, Serena smiled. Regular dog food for the wolves tonight. Kearnan was in a hurry to get back to her. Having a baby certainly hadn't diminished his sexual interest in her. If anything, he was even more insatiable than before, thank all the gods.

Pushing against the floor with her toes, Serena set the rocking chair in motion A gentle May breeze swirled around the corner of the house bringing with it the scent of newly washed pine forest and fragrant spring flowers. The baskets she had hanging from the porch rafters swayed as the softly swirling air embraced them. The spicy fragrance of herbs was added to the spring scents billowing around her.

Serena inhaled deeply. How she loved the fresh perfume of spring.

The old wolf at her feet stretched and whined.

She reached down and scratched him behind the ears. "You like spring too, don't you, Bard. The warm sun feels good on those old bones, doesn't it. Now aren't you glad you let my grandmother talk you into coming here to live? It's so much better than spending a freezing winter in snowy woods."

The wolf whined again and laid his hoary head on his paws. In his youth, he'd been a dark gray, almost black. Now, his coat had faded to a dull gray, and his head was white with age.

Serena smiled. When her grandmother had asked if Bard could come to them, both she and Kearnan had thought she'd been talking about a much younger male. But Bard was old, well past his prime. His mate had died, and he'd given over Alpha status of his pack to a younger son. Alesandra had found him wandering in the woods, cold, alone, and hungry. She'd convinced him life still had much to offer.

When George TwoBears had arrived with Bard, Kearnan had taken one look at the old wolf and declared that he would spend the cold winter months in the house with them. Another winter outside in the cold would be the death of him. And, with the birth of Morgan, it was inside the house that Bard had found his reason to live. The old wolf had taken one look at the blue-eyed, silvery-haired child with far more wolf blood than the normal werewolf and immediately declared himself her protector. Bard would have to be dead before he'd allow anyone to touch her.

Serena leaned over and stroked the old wolf's head. "You make a great baby-sitter, my old friend."

Bard licked her hand and closed his eyes.

Smiling, Serena glanced over to the old, wooden cradle rocking gently in the breeze. Complete joy welled in her heart. She'd never been so happy and content in her entire life. Morgan had been born three months ago, and Serena didn't know how she'd ever existed without her. Kearnan was just as happy, doting on Morgan to the point where their daughter reached for him as often as she wanted her mother. Nor did Bard's toothy grin intimidate her. She cooed just as happily to the wolf as she did to her mother and father, and now that she had some motor control, would grab whatever hunk of his fur was closest to her.

Serena glanced at the wolf. "Time to start dinner, Bard. Kearnan will be coming back as soon as he's finished feeding. If I don't get started, he'll 'distract' me to the point where I'll be opening cans of soup again. I'm tired of soup. So, what shall we have tonight, beef or chicken?"

Bard thumped his tail against the floor and whined. Red meat—bloody!

Chuckling, Serena nodded. "I agree. I'm hungry for red meat too. Bloody for you, but I feel like a good stew. That way it can simmer when Kearnan 'distracts" me again. Keep an eye on Morgan."

She pushed herself out of the rocking chair and turned toward the door.

Bard's full-throated growl stopped her.

She looked first into Morgan's cradle.

The baby was still sleeping, her soft lips pursed.

Serena turned her attention to Bard.

He was on his feet now, neck ruff fully flared, lips drawn back in a snarl.

Serena stepped to his side and followed the direction of his gaze.

A large, silvery-gray wolf loped across the lawn towards them. Kearnan? It looked like him, but…

Nostrils flaring, Serena inhaled, scenting the breeze. That wasn't Kearnan.

"Kearnan!" She screamed as she jerked her tee shirt over her head and slipped her sweatpants down. Dark mist swirled, and she transferred to her werewolf form.

As Serena in wolf form stepped to Bard's side at the top of the porch steps, the silver wolf slowed to a trot and finally a walk. When it reached the bottom of the steps, it stopped and sat down, ears pricked forward.

Bard growled again. Serena bared her teeth and snarled viciously.

Mist swirled, and the silver wolf assumed his human form. "Neither of you is Kearnan. I heard you call him. I need to talk to him. Where is he?" His tone was impatient and arrogant.

Serena blinked. A man who could be Kearnan's twin stood before her. The ruff on her neck rising, she snarled again. If he couldn't be polite, she didn't have to be either, even if he did look like Kearnan.

Obviously impatient, the stranger lifted his foot to start up the steps.

Serena gathered herself to leap. No way was a strange werewolf getting anywhere near her baby.

Before she could leap, a silver streak shot through the air and slammed into the stranger, knocking him to the ground. His four feet planted on opposite sides of his torso, Kearnan stood over the stranger, fangs close to his throat.

The naked stranger froze. "Damn it, Kearnan, when did you turn Alpha? I'm not going to hurt your precious wolves. Now let me up."

After another snarl, Kearnan leaped to the side and transformed. "No one gets this close to my wife and child without a warning."

"Wife and child?" The stranger pushed himself up to his feet. "Well, I'll be damned." He turned to Serena who had returned to her human form. He smiled widely as his gaze raked her naked body. *Damn, but she was one sexy werewolf.* "How did you manage to capture my reticent brother and convince him to mate you?"

Serena glanced at Kearnan. "Brother? He's your brother?"

Kearnan crossed his arms over his chest and scowled. "Serena, my brother Brendan. Brendan, Serena—and Bard. And, Serena, put your clothes on, now." His tone brooked no argument.

Wisely, Brendan pulled his gaze from Serena. Kearnan was definitely Alpha. He nodded to the wolf. *Brother, I mean no harm.*

I will rip out your throat if you make the cub so much as cry.

Brendan started then grinned at his brother. "He would, wouldn't he?"

Kearnan grinned back—ferally. "Yes. And I wouldn't stop him."

Brendan looked back at Serena who was pulling her tee-shirt over her head.

His gaze zeroed in on her breasts. “She’s lovely, Kearnan. Does she know about us?”

“Get your eyes off her breasts. And, yes, she knows about mother.”

Brendan’s nodded. “Good. Are you going to invite me in?”

“No.”

“Well, I am,” Serena stated firmly from the porch. “What’s the matter with you, Kearnan? He’s your brother.”

Kearnan glared at Brendan. “He’s my brother, but he’s a fucking pain in the ass.”

Serena cocked an eyebrow and looked at Brendan.

Kearnan’s brother clasped his hands behind his back and smiled innocently at her.

Serena stared at Brendan. He could have been Kearnan’s twin, but then they had been born in the same litter. Brendan was approximately the same height though somewhat less muscular than Kearnan. *He’s fit enough but doesn’t get as much exercise as Kearnan. That’s why his muscles aren’t quite as developed. Still, he looks like he’s in good shape—flat stomach, lean hips, nice shoulders. I’ll bet his ass is as cute.* Serena’s gaze slipped lower. *He’s hung as well as Kearnan is too.*

Serena started as Brendan’s cock twitched.

Kearnan punched his brother in the stomach and smiled with satisfaction when Brendan doubled over.

“So that’s it,” Serena said in a smug voice, “a lady’s man. Well, I’m a one man lady so keep your cock under control. Kearnan, get him some clothes. We wouldn’t want anything to happen to any dangling parts while he’s visiting. I’ll go get dinner started. We’re having beef stew, so it will take a while. You have time to catch up.”

A tiny mewl came from the cradle. Serena bent, cuddled her daughter to her chest, and went into the house.

After one last growl in Brendan's direction, Bard followed them into the house.

Straightening, Brendan grinned at his brother. "Feisty."

"Mine," Kearnan growled back.

Brendan held up both hand, palms outward. "Damn, but I seem to be doing this a lot lately. Yours. I'll not challenge you. The gods only know why, but she obviously loves you. How you managed to find her, I'll never know, but I'm glad you did. You deserve to be happy."

Slowly, Kearnan relaxed. He stuck out his hand. "Even though it's been over a year, I still wake up every now and then and can't believe how lucky I am. I had to fight her pack Alpha for her."

Brendan didn't even try to hide his surprise as he grasped Kearnan's hand. "You fought? An Alpha? You relaxed that iron will of yours?"

Grinning, Kearnan nodded. "Completely. Surprised the hell out of him—and me. Couldn't help myself. Serena was in heat. He tried to take her away. Sorry, about the attack, but when she called to me, all I heard was her fear. The wolf in me took total control."

"You let the wolf side of you take control? Damn." Brendan followed Kearnan up the steps and into the house. "You're forgiven for the attack. I'd have done the same, I guess. Did you tell Serena about Mother before or after you were mated?"

"Of course. I wouldn't mate her without telling her."

Brendan ducked the punch Kearnan had aimed at his head. "Sorry. Guess I should know better than to ask such a stupid question. Too much time spent with humans, I guess. So, Serena didn't want to go even after you told her about Mother?"

Kearnan led the way to the second floor. Once in his room, he pulled some jeans and a shirt out of a drawer for

Brendan. "She thought about it, then informed me in no uncertain terms that she didn't give a damn. Boxers?"

"Silk, if you have them. What about…"

"My phobia about being too violent in bed for a woman, even a werewolf?" Kearnan finished as he handed the clothing to Brendan then dug out more for himself.

"Clarisse was a real bitch," Brendan answered.

"Serena proved I wouldn't hurt her."

Brendan noted the soft smile on his brother's lips. Kearnan was finally happy with both himself and his life. "That's a story I'd like to hear."

Kearnan grinned at him as he buttoned his jeans. "It's a story you won't hear. But I will tell you this. You really want to find a woman who knows how to use her teeth. Now, why are you here?"

"Dad married a human. She's expecting twins."

Before Kearnan could do more than begin to stutter, the smile disappeared from Brendan's face. "And Belle's gone. She's disappeared."

* * * * *

"So let me get this straight," Serena said as they ate dinner. "Your sister Belle has spent the last ten years taking care of your father..."

"Belle didn't really take care of him," Brendan interrupted, "not in the sense that he needed someone to clean up after him, feed him or bathe him. She just..."

"Stayed with him because you were all afraid he'd try to commit suicide," Serena finished after another mouthful of beef stew. When Brendan stopped chewing, she continued, "Kearnan told me the entire story. Why her and not one of the rest of you?"

When neither of them answered, Serena muttered something about stupid men under her breath then continued, "Anyway, your father has found a new mate, right?"

Brendan nodded.

"Well, hell," Serena snapped. "I'd disappear too."

Kearnan stared at his wife.

Brendan's fork stopped half way to his mouth.

"What did you expect her to do?" Serena continued in an irritated voice. "After ten years, she's finally able to take some real time for herself and not worry about what could happen if she's not there every single minute. I don't blame her. I'd have done the same thing."

"But what if something has happened to her?"

Kearnan frowned. "Has there been any trouble with anyone? Has Belle been bothered?"

Brendan shook his head. "No. It's just that she's never done anything like this before. She's always told me or Father where she was going and when she'd be back."

Serena snorted. "Stupid Alpha control freaks," she mumbled into her spoon.

Kearnan grinned. "You'll have to forgive Serena, Brendan. She's made running away and hiding from her family an art form. Remind me to tell you about it someday."

"But what about Belle?"

Kearnan pushed his empty plate away. "I think Serena's right. Belle has basically been at Father's beck and call for the last ten years. He doesn't need her anymore. She has the right to take some time for herself."

Brendan's voice was laced with worry. "But not without telling someone where she's going."

Kearnan leaned forward. "Do you know where Garth is?"

Brendan snorted. "Half the time Garth doesn't know where Garth is."

Kearnan laced his fingers together. "What about Melody? When was the last time you heard from her?"

Brendan shook his head. "You know Melody comes and goes as she likes."

"Then why shouldn't Belle?" Serena interjected.

A low cry came though the baby monitor.

Serena rose. "Morgan's waking up. Would you like to meet your niece?"

Brendan smiled. "Only if you promise me Bard won't tear my throat out if she cries."

"Oh, I think I can promise you that, if you behave yourself," she answered with a grin. "I'll be back as soon as I change her."

Both men watched Serena leave. Pushing his chair away from the table, Kearnan asked, "Do you want to wash or dry?"

"Wash or dry what?"

"The dishes, of course," Kearnan answered with big grin on his face. Brendan hadn't washed or dried a dish in years.

"Me—dry dishes! No fucking way."

Kearnan shrugged. "Okay, you can wash them. Would you like an apron?"

The appalled look on Brendan's face was priceless. "Apron?"

Kearnan continued grinning. "Oh yeah, you're wearing my jeans not one of your custom made suits. It's okay if you slop some water on them."

Speechless, Brendan allowed Kearnan to push him to the sink. As he filled it with hot water and dish liquid, Kearnan cleared the table. Then, Brendan smiled to himself. It was good to see Kearnan so happy.

Brendan placed a bowl on the floor under Bard's nose.

The old wolf sniffed then licked it clean. *Thank you.*

"Polite old wolf, isn't he. How'd he end up here?"

Kearnan cocked an eyebrow as he dumped some dishes into the sink. "This *is* a wolf preserve. And don't let Serena see you giving him table scraps. She doesn't want him eating too much 'human' food. Says it's unhealthy for him."

"What Serena doesn't know won't hurt her, will it Bard?"

The old wolf's tail beat against the floor twice.

Kearnan grinned. "Just because you give him food now doesn't mean he still won't try to bite your hand off if you make Morgan cry. Now, tell me about Dad's new mate."

Brendan soaped a bowl then rinsed it and handed it to Kearnan. "Moira Archer. She's a perfume chemist, a damned good one. She worked for the perfume company we were going to go into partnership with."

Kearnan put the dry dish in the cupboard. "Were?"

Brendan shrugged. "What do we need with the company when we have their best chemist."

Kearnan grinned. "Dad always was a sly bastard. How'd he talk her into leaving them?"

Brendan handed his brother another dish. "He didn't. She was in heat when we met her, and he pretty much demanded that she go with him. She did."

Kearnan faced his brother. "But human heat isn't that compelling to us."

"She's got some werewolf blood, and she was wearing perfume with an aconite base," Brendan added. "Damn but her scent was enticing. I wanted her myself. Thought Dad was going to challenge me right there in front of two hundred people."

"Dad? Challenge? You!"

Brendan shook his head. "Yeah, who'd have believed it. Take my advice. Don't underestimate Dad's fighting skills. He took out the two goons who kidnapped Moira without even breaking a sweat."

Kearnan didn't even pretend to dry the dish in his hand. "Moira was kidnapped?"

"And after he kicked ass, Dad would have mounted her right there in front of me. I left."

"She accepted his dominance?"

Brendan grinned. "Yeah, and you should have seen the look on her face. If he hadn't mounted her then and there, I think she would have jumped him."

Kearnan shook his head. "She must be one hell of a woman. I'm glad Dad found her."

"Me too. With him happy and taking a real interest in the business, I can start expanding the way I want to."

Kearnan grinned. This was the Brendan he knew—ready to conquer the world.

Then, Brendan scowled. "Kearnan, about Belle."

Kearnan put an arm around Brendan's shoulders. "Serena's right. After all those years with Father, she needed some time to herself. She's fine. Don't worry. I'm sure you'll be hearing from her anytime now."

"Yeah, you're probably right," Brendan agreed. "Now get your arm off me and finish drying those dishes. I want to meet my niece."

Fifteen minutes later, Serena entered the kitchen. After a low growl in Brendan's direction, the old wolf eased himself down onto a multicolored hooked rug next to her.

"Told you that bribe wouldn't work," Kearnan muttered out of the side of his mouth.

Serena settled into a chair and turned the baby to face Brendan. "Say hello to your Uncle Brendan, love."

Leaning forward, Brendan stared into the baby's face. "She's pretty. You better save your strength, brother. Once she's old enough to mate, you'll have to fight the males off."

Serena snorted. "As if she won't be capable of taking care of herself."

Brendan leaned closer.

Morgan screwed up her face and let out a howl.

Jerking back, Brendan rubbed his left ear. "She's got a good set of lungs on her."

With a tired smile, Serena sighed. "She's hungry again. Honestly, she's going to be a regular butter ball if she keeps eating like this."

Pulling up her shirt, Serena guided her daughter's mouth to her nipple.

Brendan froze. *Gods, but she had a beautiful breast. And the color of her nipple – cinnamon. That was it. Did it taste as spicy?*

A snarl and punch in the shoulder from Kearnan had Brendan staggering across the kitchen. "Keep your eyes away from my wife's breasts."

"Kind of hard to do when she flashes me," Brendan snarled back.

Serena's nostrils flared. "Flash you. Are you nuts? I'm feeding my baby. Don't tell me you haven't seen a naked breast before."

Brendan looked from one angry face to another. How did he keep getting himself into these fixes? "Look, I'm sorry. Women in New York just don't go around nursing babies in public. I haven't seen a baby sucking on a breast since we left the pack."

He glanced back at Kearnan.

His brother's eyes had returned to their normal silver color.

Brendan turned his attention to Serena. Her lips were still pinched together. *Damn, but flashing may not have been the best word to use.* "Well hell, Serena. Of course, I've seen naked breasts before. It's just that yours are more beautiful than any others I've ever seen."

The growl behind him told Brendan that Kearnan wasn't particularly happy with his answer, but Serena's reaction was more important. Even as Alpha as his brother had become, Brendan had a feeling that his pretty, black-haired mate pretty much had Kearnan wrapped around her elegant fingers.

Serena's lips relaxed then twitched into a smile. "You certainly have a silver tongue to match you hair and eyes, don't you Brendan? You probably have women falling at your feet."

Brendan grinned and allowed his gaze to drop to Serena's breast once more, ducking when he heard his brother's arm begin to swing. With another duck and quick feint, Brendan put the table between himself and Kearnan. Holding up his hands, he said, "I know. Yours. I concede. You can't blame a werewolf for dreaming, can you?"

Scowling, Kearnan fisted his hands on his hips. "Dream about the breasts of some other man's wife. Those belong to me."

Chuckling, Serena switched her daughter to her other breast. Grabbing a dishtowel, she draped it over her shoulder. "There. How's that. No more free show."

Hand over his heart, Brendan sighed.

Before he could say anything, Kearnan growled, "If you start spouting poetry, I'm throwing you out, and you can sleep in the forest tonight."

Brendan turned a hang dog look Serena's way. "Can you see what I was forced to endure as I was growing up? Kearnan has no appreciation for the finer things in life, good wine, the theater, museums. Instead he buries himself in the woods. Say the word, Serena, and I'll sweep you away to real civilization."

Serena's laughter was the only thing that kept Kearnan from attacking his brother then and there.

"Brendan, you better shut up before Kearnan rips your head off, and not the one on top of your neck."

Grinning, Brendan bowed. "Welcome to the family, Serena. You're good for Kearnan. I'm glad my brother found you—and your beautiful breasts."

Enjoy an excerpt from:

BRIANNA

Celestial Passions

ℬ

Groaning, Brianna opened her eyes then gasped at the sudden ache in her shoulder. Befuddled at first, she tried to focus her eyes in the dim light. Frowning, she lifted her head and looked around. Where was she? The last thing she remembered, she'd been in that clearing with the aliens.

Her eyes widened. Aliens—and soldiers.

A memory of Mark pointing a gun at her appeared before her eyes.

Her temper flared. "That son of a bitch! He shot me! What the hell did I ever do to him? He was the one who tried to *rape* me!"

Again she looked around the small room. Nothing looked familiar. *Where* was she? She continued to search her memory.

A bright beam of light. Miklan! He'd grabbed her wrist and pulled her into that bright light.

She felt the blood drain from her face. *My God, I must be on a spaceship.*

Heart leaping into her throat, Brianna gasped and choked. Shivers raced up and down her body. A spaceship? Oh God! What was she going to do?

Gritting her teeth, she forced herself to slow her panicked breathing. Fists clenched, she reasserted command over her trembling body. "I will not panic. I will not lie here shaking and crying like some too stupid to live heroine in a bad romance novel. I can handle this. I *will* handle this!"

She sat up and immediately grimaced at the twinge of pain in her shoulder. How badly had she been hurt? Moving slowly, she carefully raised her arms and legs. They moved the way they were supposed to, although there was a definite tenderness in her right shoulder.

Except for the white bandage covering her wound, she was naked. "Where the hell are my clothes?"

Wrapping the blanket around her torso, Brianna swung her legs over the bunk and pushed herself to her feet. Moving carefully, she gained her equilibrium and worked the slight stiffness out of her legs. How long had she been unconscious?

Brianna pulled the blanket more tightly beneath her arms and walked to the door. Tentatively, she placed her palm upon the handprint in the middle. It slid open with a slight whisper, revealing an empty room.

When she stepped cautiously into the larger room, the quiet hiss of the door closing caused her to spin about. A handprint identical to that on the inside was also affixed to this side. Pressing her palm against it, she was relieved when the door glided open. At least she could get back in. But was it a refuge or a cage?

Turning once more, Brianna took stock of her surroundings. This room was much larger with sparse but what looked like comfortable furnishings. A table with ten chairs was to one side while a sofa, overstuffed chair, and a smaller table sat on the other side. A large plant, with pale blue leaves and flowers of a darker blue, stood next to a closed door to her right. However, the huge window on the opposite wall drew her attention. There were drapes of a sort, pulled open. And outside of the window was nothing, absolutely nothing.

Brianna staggered to the window, braced her hands against it, and gaped at the blackness. One tiny pinpoint of light could be seen far, far below, but it flickered out as she stared at it. "Oh my God," she moaned, "I *am* in a spaceship! Where's Earth? How do I get home?" Frozen in place, her thoughts a whirling maelstrom, she didn't hear the door slide open behind her.

Rubbing his chin as he walked into the room—he really needed to shave—his eyes were immediately drawn to the figure standing before the window. Stopping half way across the room, he stared at the woman who had danced erotically through his dreams for the last week. She stood with her back to him, a blanket covering her from her torso to her knees. Her fiery hair cascaded to her hips.

A mental picture of those soft flames wrapped around his body jumped into his mind.

"So, you have finally awakened."

Brianna tensed. She wasn't alone. She turned slowly and gasped in shock. The man who shared the room with her was completely naked. A picture of Miklan and Cindar as they lay naked and unconscious on the lab tables leaped into her mind. In many ways, this man was much like them. He had the same skin tone, almond-shaped eyes, thin nose, and lips. His ears were pointed and his hair, though longer, thicker, and a darker brown, looked just as silky. He stood taller than Miklan, only a few inches short of seven feet. There, however, the similarities ended.

A colorful tattoo of what looked like some sort of dragon rode high on his right shoulder. His well-developed chest tapered to a slender waist. His legs were long and also displayed more muscle than Miklan's.

Most obvious, though, was the difference in his genitals. A long, thick penis rested in a nest of fine brown pubic hair. He had a tail. She could see it dangling between his legs. But it really was a tail, not an elongated penis. This man was definitely not a hermaphrodite!

As Brianna watched, his penis stirred and began to rise.

Fear blossomed, and she pressed back against the window. She jerked her gaze back up his body to meet dark eyes surrounded by thick lashes, eyes that did not attempt to hide their amusement—or interest. Beautiful white teeth flashed as both hands combed his hair behind his ears. Muscles rippled across his naked chest as he spoke.

"You're a very beautiful woman."

She swallowed and clutched her blanket more tightly. The musical language was the same as Miklan's, but the voice much richer, much deeper, much more…masculine.

More importantly, she couldn't understand a word he said.

Her imagination fueling her growing panic, Brianna flattened herself against the window. What was he saying to her? Would he understand her like Miklan did? Why was he naked? What was she doing here? Had she been kidnapped for sex? Were all those lurid stories about alien sex in those trashy tabloids true?

He spoke again. "Come, make love with me. Wrap your hair around my body as I suck your beautiful breasts. When I finally enter you, you will scream with pleasure."

Brianna had no idea what he had said, but she sagged with relief when he turned away. She continued to watch him warily as he strode to a panel attached to the wall, punched a button, and spoke into what looked like an intercom, undoubtedly about her. Was he calling Miklan? Please, let Miklan come.

In a few minutes, the light above a door flashed. When it opened, a woman, at least a person that *looked* like a woman, walked in and began talking to the man. Brianna was unable to follow their conversation, but they were obviously talking about her. What amazed her was the nonchalance they both showed towards his nudity. Did these people just walk around naked? God, what had she gotten herself into?

Why an electronic book?

We live in the Information Age—an exciting time in the history of human civilization, in which technology rules supreme and continues to progress in leaps and bounds every minute of every day. For a multitude of reasons, more and more avid literary fans are opting to purchase e-books instead of paper books. The question from those not yet initiated into the world of electronic reading is simply: *Why?*

1. ***Price.*** An electronic title at Ellora's Cave Publishing and Cerridwen Press runs anywhere from 40% to 75% less than the cover price of the exact same title in paperback format. Why? Basic mathematics and cost. It is less expensive to publish an e-book (no paper and printing, no warehousing and shipping) than it is to publish a paperback, so the savings are passed along to the consumer.
2. ***Space.*** Running out of room in your house for your books? That is one worry you will never have with electronic books. For a low one-time cost, you can purchase a handheld device specifically designed for e-reading. Many e-readers have large, convenient screens for viewing. Better yet, hundreds of titles can be stored within your new library—on a single microchip. There are a variety of e-readers from different manufacturers. You can also read e-books on your PC or laptop computer. (Please note that Ellora's Cave does not endorse any specific brands.

You can check our websites at www.ellorascave.com or www.cerridwenpress.com for information we make available to new consumers.)

3. ***Mobility***. Because your new e-library consists of only a microchip within a small, easily transportable e-reader, your entire cache of books can be taken with you wherever you go.
4. ***Personal Viewing Preferences.*** Are the words you are currently reading too small? Too large? Too... *ANNOYING*? Paperback books cannot be modified according to personal preferences, but e-books can.
5. ***Instant Gratification.*** Is it the middle of the night and all the bookstores near you are closed? Are you tired of waiting days, sometimes weeks, for bookstores to ship the novels you bought? Ellora's Cave Publishing sells instantaneous downloads twenty-four hours a day, seven days a week, every day of the year. Our webstore is never closed. Our e-book delivery system is 100% automated, meaning your order is filled as soon as you pay for it.

Those are a few of the top reasons why electronic books are replacing paperbacks for many avid readers.

As always, Ellora's Cave and Cerridwen Press welcome your questions and comments. We invite you to email us at Comments@ellorascave.com or write to us directly at Ellora's Cave Publishing Inc., 1056 Home Avenue, Akron, OH 44310-3502.

Cerridwen, the Celtic Goddess of wisdom, was the muse who brought inspiration to storytellers and those in the creative arts. Cerridwen Press encompasses the best and most innovative stories in all genres of today's fiction. Visit our site and discover the newest titles by talented authors who still get inspired - much like the ancient storytellers did, once upon a time.

ELLORA'S CAVE
ROMANTICA PUBLISHING

2395610

Made in the USA